Christmas with Angel

Christmas with Angel

BY

LEXI POST

Christmas with Angel
Last Chance Series Book #1

Sequel to *Cowboy's Match: Poker Flat Series #2*
Prequel to *Trace's Trouble: Last Chance Series #2*

Copyright © 2015 by Lexi Post

This book is a work of fiction. The names, characters, places, and incidents are products of the writer's imagination or have been used fictitiously and are not to be construed as real. Any resemblance to persons, living or dead, actual events, locales or organizations is entirely coincidental.

ALL RIGHTS RESERVED. No part of this book may be used or reproduced in any manner whatsoever without written permission from the author.

First Print Edition
Print ISBN: 978-0-9967980-5-1

For information contact Lexi Post at
www.lexipostbooks.com

Cover design by Bella Media Management
(http://www.bellamediamanagement.com/)

Cover photo: Cover Me, Becky McGraw
(https://www.facebook.com/CoverMePhotog?fref=ts)

Christmas with Angel

(Last Chance Series, Book #1)

By Lexi Post

Cowboy firefighter, Cole Hatcher, is determined to do what's right and take his fiancé with him to his mother's annual Christmas dinner party. After all, she *is* his mother and the rest of the family will be there.

Lacey Winters can't forgive her future mother-in-law for keeping her and Cole apart for eight years. While she loves Cole's family, including the five they are living with, she wants to spend Christmas alone with Cole on Last Chance Ranch.

But there are worse things brewing than family drama. This Christmas day, nothing goes as planned…for anyone.

Acknowledgments

For Chief Robert Fabich, Sr., who once again came through with his expertise. Thank you for all your patience as you taught me about house fires.

And for my sister Paige Wood, whose advice is invaluable to me as well as her expert abilities.

For my critique partner, Marie Patrick, who was integral in getting this book to publication, as was Merritt Crowder, my dear friend from St. Croix who has the eye of an eagle when it comes to reading.

Thank you all for supporting my crazy idea of writing a glimpse into Cole and Lacey's happily ever after.

Christmas with Angel: Last Chance Series Book #1 is a "bridge" book. It is the sequel to *Cowboy's Match: Poker Flat Series Book #2* and the prequel to *Trace's Trouble: Last Chance Series Book #2*. The Poker Flat Series was inspired by Bret Harte's short story, *The Outcasts of Poker Flat*, first published in 1869. In Harte's story, four members of Poker Flat society—a gambler, a prostitute, a madam, and a drunk--are banned from the western settlement when a sudden urge to be virtuous overtakes the citizens. On their way to the next settlement, the outcasts stop to rest at the base of some high mountains. An innocent couple, a young man and his fiancée (a tavern waitress), comes down from the mountains and rests with them. This cast of characters explores the relationship between the innocent and the tainted in Harte's story.

In *Cowboy's Match,* the story asks the question, what is tainted and what is innocent? In *Christmas with Angel* the question becomes, can some be less "tainted" than others, and when all is said and done, does perspective play a role in the determination?

Chapter One

Last Chance Ranch, Arizona

December 23rd

Cole Hatcher added two pillows to the makeshift bed of sleeping bags on the hay. He'd unzipped each and spread them out so he and Lacey could crawl in together. Maybe if they could have a little privacy, they could settle their Christmas issue.

He'd pilfered all the snowflake decorations from the tree inside and hung them from the beams. In his mind, he'd envisioned it to look like it was snowing, but in reality, it looked like plastic, glass and felt snowflakes hanging from beams. Lacey would get it though. She couldn't expect more than this from her cowboy.

Adjusting the garland around the stall walls, he pulled over the small table he used for grooming the horses and placed it next to the bed. With a rag he'd grabbed from the house, he wiped it off and placed a bottle of wine on it with two plastic cups. "That should do it." His Christmas Eve present was ready, though a few hours early.

Stuffing the rag in his back pocket, he turned the battery-operated lantern to low and set it next to the wine. "Perfect."

As he headed out of the barn, the six horses in residence paid him no heed except for Angel. Her wary eyes watched him until he was out of sight.

Giving Angel to Lacey had been the best thing he'd done for that horse, besides take her from her owner. She was so fearful of men that her bond with Lacey had grown strong.

Now if he could just get his fiancé onto the same page with him, life would be great again.

Cole strode across the dirt yard, the only sound to break the crisp night air, the two note call of a whippoorwill. The quiet beckoned him, but he needed Lacey to truly enjoy it. The house lights should have been welcoming but with his two cousins in residence, one baby, Billy and his grandparents, the four bedroom house was packed.

He took the stairs to the porch two at a time. Pulling back the screen door, he opened the heavy, ironwood front door. As he stepped in, he had to stop himself from stepping back out.

The baby cried upstairs while his two cousins, Logan and Trace argued. A door slammed on the upper level then Trace stomped down the stairs, yelling back over his shoulder, "I'll be watching the game with Grandpa if you come to your senses!" He nodded to Cole as he passed by.

Old Billy, who used to work and live at Poker Flat and had just spent two months in rehab for alcoholism, ambled through the front hall from the kitchen, a bottle of water in his hand and a smile on his face. The television in the living room clicked on just as Billy entered and the volume increased substantially.

Cole winced, the noise level and activity in the house was almost painful. Like Lacey, he couldn't wait for their own home to be completed, but it barely had walls and was far too incomplete for them to have the privacy and quiet they needed. Since Lacey had given up her casita at the Poker Flat Nudist Resort, they had nowhere to go… except the barn.

She was probably in their room where she always retreated right after dinner to crunch numbers, do research, or iron clothes for work. He ran up the stairs, excited to show her the present he'd arranged, and opened the door to the bedroom.

Lacey stood next to the bed, her deep pink sweater fitting her like a second-skin, wisps of blonde hair escaping her long braid. Her maroon skirt flowed about her, accentuating her delicate femininity. He still couldn't believe this hot woman was his. She had a basket of laundry dumped out on their bed, clean clothes strewn over the quilt and a small pile folded to her right. He walked straight to her and wrapped his arms around her waist from behind. "I have a surprise for you."

She stilled then sighed. "Is it ear plugs?"

He kissed her neck beneath her ear, loving how tiny she felt against him. "Even better."

She dropped his fire department t-shirt and turned in his arms. "Better is good." She lifted her arms around his neck. "Don't get me wrong. I love your family. There just seems to be so many of them in this particular house. And now that Billy's here, it makes it very cramped."

He looked into her light brown eyes that reminded him of amaretto. "You love my family? Even my parents?"

She lowered her lashes and stared at his chest.

Damn, he needed to wait to discuss that. Talking about his parents only brought up what his mother had done to break them apart. That didn't set the mood he wanted. He wouldn't press it now. "So aren't you a little bit curious about my surprise?"

She lifted her gaze to meet his. "Is this my Christmas Eve present?"

His family had always exchanged gifts on Christmas day, but maybe he and Lacey could start their own tradition. "Yes, just a few hours early."

She looked over her shoulder at the clock sitting on the nightstand. "Only three hours and seventeen minutes early. Should I wait?"

He started to grin but it turned to a grimace as his

cousin's baby let out an ear-piercing wail. "You might be able to, but I can't."

At the sound of the baby's scream, Lacey buried her head against his chest. She lifted it to look up at him. "I could use a surprise right about now."

"Good." He kissed her on the forehead then let her go so he could take her hand. As he took a step toward the door, she resisted. "I thought you were going to give me a surprise."

"We have to go outside for this."

She pointed to the pile of clothes. "But I need to finish folding the laundry."

"Leave them. This is more important."

"Okay." She let him pull her down the hall.

When they got to the top of the stairs, he released her hand and stepped aside so she could descend first. Another screeching wail sounded from above, and they both picked up their pace. As he opened the front door, the television volume increased another decimal in the living room and from the corner of his eye he caught sight of Billy who had joined his grandfather and Trace.

Lacey stepped onto the porch and sighed.

No sooner had he closed the door than she placed her hand on his chest. "Do you hear that?"

He listened. The quiet was almost deafening until four hoots, sounding like a bouncing ball, broke the silence. "You mean the Screech Owl?"

She smiled slyly. "No, I mean the quiet."

He grinned. "Wait until you see my surprise." He took her hand and they walked down the steps toward the barn.

"I hope you didn't get me another horse. I'm very attached to Angel and I think she'd get jealous."

He shook his head. "No, it's not a horse. Luckily, I haven't had any calls this week. Maybe the Christmas spirit has people being kinder to their animals." He frowned at the thought of what else the Christmas season brought. "Now if we could just get Christmas tree fires under control, everyone could have a happy Christmas."

She squeezed his hand. "I've never understood the need for a live evergreen tree in the Arizona desert. It's so dry. If a person wants to smell evergreens, they can always go up to Prescott for the day or take a hike right here in our own mountains."

"You make the house smell great with those scented candles you use. I'm glad you found them in the glass jars."

She stopped at the entrance to the barn and looked at him. "Can you turn off the firefighter tonight and give me the cowboy who loves to save abused, hurt, and unwanted horses?"

He grinned sheepishly. "I'll try. Actually, your surprise is definitely from the cowboy." He winked.

Lacey's gaze roamed over him, and he couldn't help but count himself lucky all over again. To have found her a second time, at a fire no less, had been sheer luck. That she was just as dedicated to his horse rescue ranch as he was, was a bonus. Her wizardry with the finances had also improved their solvency. But to have captured her heart once more against all odds was the greatest luck of all. "If you keep looking at me like that, your surprise might have to wait."

She widened her eyes. "Like what?" She even batted her lashes.

He laughed and pulled her into his embrace. "I love you, soon-to-be Lacey Hatcher."

"I know." She stood on tiptoe to give him a kiss.

When she didn't deepen the kiss, he had to stop himself from lowering his lips to hers again. The open barn door was not the place to start making love to his woman. Reluctantly, he released her, but grasped her hand again.

After pulling the large door closed behind him, he led Lacey through the barn, passing the filled stalls until she slowed by Angel. He understood and let go, continuing toward the last stall, not wanting to disturb the bond between her and the rescued horse.

No sooner had Lacey turned toward the white Arabian, than Angel gave a soft nicker and walked to the stall door. Lacey pet the badly marred head, cooing to her like one would talk with a baby.

Cole never tired of watching their connection. He had almost given up hope that Angel would ever interact with humans again after the abuse she'd take from her former owner. That the horse came into his life shortly after he had found Lacey again made him think it was fate. Though the horse shied away from men, she completely trusted Lacey.

When Lacey finished, she walked slowly toward him, or was she sauntering toward him? Shit, his muscles tensed in anticipation.

She still wore her clothes from work, her long skirt swishing against her white cowboy boots. The sweater showed off her figure even if it didn't reveal even a hint of cleavage. It was hard to believe she worked at a nudist resort. He was thankful once again that the resort had a strict policy about employees keeping their clothes on during work. He would go insane if Lacey was supposed to work nude. On the other hand, because Kendra owned the nudist resort she was expected to be nude. He had no idea how Wade handled his fiancé being naked half the day. Cole couldn't do it.

But Lacey was sexy even with her clothes on, especially after a long day, when her braid had loosened and her messy wheat-colored hair made it look as if she'd just spent an hour in bed with him.

He watched her eyes closely as she approached. Her gaze was riveted to him and his chest puffed with pride. When she licked her lips, he had to force himself to stay still as every tendon pushed at him to move.

Finally, her gaze flitted to the stall behind him and her lips formed a pleased smile. "Oh Cole, it's the best present you could have given me."

He released the breath he'd been holding and opened his arms. "You like it?"

She walked straight into his embrace. "I love it."

"It might get a little chilly tonight."

She shrugged. "That's why I have you to keep me warm."

"Just to keep you warm?" He frowned. "I was hoping to start a fire inside you."

Lacey's short intake of breath had his cock taking notice.

She wrapped her arms around his neck. "You are as good at starting fires as putting them out."

"Only for you." He lowered his head and kissed her.

She pressed her body against him and pushed her tongue between his lips. He caught it with his own.

Every nook of her mouth was like new territory. He tasted the tartness of the wine she had with dinner and a flavor that was all Lacey. His hands roamed over her back, feeling her sweater slide against silk.

His cock hardened at the thought of what his Racy Lacey might be wearing underneath.

She pulled her lips away abruptly. "You have too many clothes on."

"I was thinking the same about you." He wiggled his brow. "I bet I can take my shirt off faster than you can." He let his arm go slack in anticipation of the race. They were always betting about sex.

She kept her arms around him. "And what does the winner get?"

"I'm thinking, choice of position." At his words, a shiver ran through her body, sending lightening straight to his balls.

"On the count of three. One. Two. Three."

No sooner had she dropped her arms than he reached back and pulled his flannel over his head. One button pinged across the stall, hitting the wood, as his face cleared the tail of the shirt.

Lacey had brought the sweater up over her head, but her face was still hidden.

Cole stared at the pale pink corset that cupped her breasts and accentuated her waist and hips. With her skirt still on, she looked like a saloon girl from the old west.

As she pulled the sweater free, she took a breath and her areolas peeked above their confines.

He swallowed hard.

"Are you admiring my new corset?" She smiled slyly, the vixen.

He shook his head as he traced a finger along the top edge of the satiny lingerie. "No, I'm admiring this." He pushed his finger inside the cup and flicked at the hard nipple beneath."

"But you like it, right?"

"I think it might require a closer inspection." He used his other hand to burrow beneath her other cup and lift the breast above the soft satin so the corset held it up for him to view her rosy tip. "Hmm, I'm liking it more and more." He performed the same readjustment on her other breast then stood back. "Now that's perfect." He stared at her hard nipples held aloft. "I really like it."

"I'm glad." Her lips formed a seductive pout. "But I lost the bet."

He reached out one hand and brushed his fingertips across her hard nipples. "Yes, you did."

Her chest rose as she sucked in a breath at his touch.

He loved how responsive she was. "I think it's time you took off your skirt so I can decide exactly what position I want you in."

She cocked her head. "And that must be determined by what I'm wearing underneath my skirt?"

He nodded. His soon-to-be wife never failed to surprise him when they crawled into bed at night. Her love of lingerie had him anticipating their alone time even during dinner. He was definitely the beneficiary of that little fetish. It didn't take much to get Lacey hot, but in the house, she had to keep quiet when they made love, and that took something away from the experience for her. Tonight, she could let go completely with no one the wiser.

Lacey untied the bow at her waist and pushed the skirt down to the barn floor before stepping out of it.

He was too distracted by the movement of her breasts at first, to understand her smile.

"So what position would you like?" Her voice was teasing, a sound he hadn't heard in over a month.

This had definitely been needed. He lowered his gaze and raised his brows. "I can't decide until you take off that damn slip too."

She giggled, another sound he hadn't heard in a while. He needed to do something about that. The stress of building a house, working, caring for the horses with so much family around was too stressful for the only-child Lacey.

As she shimmied out of her slip, his jaw dropped and his cock hardened.

Chapter Two

Cole's proper, no-swearing, always sweet Lacey stood before him in white cowboy boots, white lace stockings that rose to her thighs where they hooked to the corset. The satin of the lingerie came to the tip of her mons where a ribbon on each side of her folds snaked its way between her legs. He swallowed hard. "Turn around."

She did, slowly, stopping when her back was completely to him.

Shit, she could turn him on as easy as striking a match. The two ribbons had turned into one somewhere between her legs and that one hooked onto the back of the satin corset. Her round ass cheeks begged him to grab them and thrust inside her tight sheath, but he held himself back and simply enjoyed the view.

That's when he noticed something odd about her crease. "Lacey, what do you have between your legs?" His stomach dropped. If she had a bullet vibrator inside her then he'd know he had been seriously failing her.

She looked over her shoulder worriedly. "It was supposed to be a surprise."

He forced a smile. "So surprise me."

She bent forward and spread her legs.

He took a step closer as his heart started to race. There was something attached to the ribbon that lay along her crease. Unable to resist touching her, he spread her ass cheeks, his dark tanned hands a stark contrast against her paler skin, and his cock grew painfully hard. His voice was gruff when he spoke. "What is it?"

She looked back at him, her forehead creased in worry. "It's a small butt plug. Adriana said—"

"I bet she did."

"You don't like it?"

He forced his hands to let go of her ass while he tried to gain control of his raging need. "Not like it? Shit Lacey, it's so fucking hot, I'm going to come before I get inside you."

"Really?" Her smile was hopeful as she wiggled her butt before him.

He grabbed it to stop her. "Is that what you want? For me to come all over your ass instead of inside you?"

She straightened quickly. "No."

He let her break his hold as she turned around. Just knowing she had the butt plug inside her, that it would press against him as he entered her, had him fisting his hands, trying to control his need.

"Adriana said you would like it."

He rolled his eyes. Adriana Perez, former prostitute and current bartender at Poker Flat Nudist Resort where Lacey worked, had already educated his relatively innocent fiancée on a number of sex toys. Sometimes he didn't know whether to thank the woman or strangle her. His ardor cooled at the implications of Lacey's outfit and accoutrements.

"Did you wear that at work all day?"

Her smile faded. "Oh no. I wasn't sure if I would like it, so I slipped it in after dinner. I used the lubricant she told me to get. It was going to be my Christmas Eve present to you if I liked it."

"Do you like it?"

She twisted her hips about. "I think so. But Adriana said the best part was when you push inside me."

Cole closed his eyes and took a deep breath, counting to ten on the inhale and then exhale. When he opened his eyes, Lacey was clasping her hands in front of her, hiding her mons from his view, a sure indication she was unsure.

He grasped her shoulders. "Lacey, that is the hottest outfit and sexual toy you have worn to date, and I'm just trying not to come before I can give you the pleasure you deserve."

Her face relaxed and she wrapped her arms around him, resting her head on his chest, her breasts crushing against his skin. "I'm so glad. I really want to see what it's like."

He released her shoulders and hugged her to him, his

cock anxious to be let loose to dive into his woman. From habit, he reached down with one hand and grasped her ass to pull her tighter against him and his thumb slipped under the ribbon.

"Oh." Lacey pulled her head away to look at him. "It tingles when you do that."

"Do what? This?" He purposefully pulled at the lifeline to the butt plug.

"Oh Gosh." Lacey's hands grasped his waist even as she arched her back.

If he didn't still have his jeans on, he would have come all over her by now and if that's what it took to give her pleasure then he'd keep them on. He gently tugged the pink ribbon again.

Lacey pushed her ass backward, begging for more.

He pulled away from her and sat on a hay bale he'd set up by the side of the makeshift bed. It had just been delivered that day and along with its mates gave the stall a sweet, earthy scent. "Come here." He patted one of his legs.

She didn't question him. Ever since the popsicle night at Poker Flat, she'd been more than willing to trust him with her sexual explorations. Lacey sat sideways on his leg.

He chuckled. "No, Racy Lacey. Straddle my leg and face away from me."

Despite her frown, she did as he requested. With an arm around her waist, he pulled her tight against him, knowing full well it would move that pink ribbon.

"Cole, if you keep doing that I'm going to come."

He grinned behind her head and breathed in her clean-linen scent, enjoying the softness of her hair on his face. "And what if I do this?"

Keeping her anchored to him, he brought one hand up and rolled her left nipple between his thumb and forefinger.

"Ah." Lacey let her head fall against him.

He moved his other hand up to give the right nipple equal attention. His gorgeous woman arched her back, pressing her breasts into his touch.

He chuckled silently, loving how much she enjoyed his hands on her. Gently, he clamped her nipples between his fingers. When she pulled back against him, he didn't let go, allowing her to determine the exact pressure she liked.

"Cole."

"Yes?" When she didn't say anything more, he let go of her tight nubs and anchored one arm around her again. With his other hand, he smoothed down the pink satin on her torso until he reached her mons, lightly covered with golden-blonde curls. He couldn't see where he was, but he could imagine, and like a blind person, let his hand explore her folds.

Wetness coated his fingers and he smiled into her hair. She was so ready, she made his cock painfully hard. As much as he wanted to release it from its confines, he refused to until he brought her to her first, of what he hoped would be, many orgasms of the night.

Lacey started to make short moaning sounds deep in her throat, causing his balls to tighten.

Shit. As much as he wanted to play with her more, he had to bring her to release.

Quickly, he moved his fingers from teasing her opening to her clit and rubbed it upward. She always enjoyed that stroke.

And he wasn't wrong. Her hips started to rock against his busy hand, which pulled on the pink ribbon strapped to the butt plug.

"Oh gosh, Cole."

He tried to ignore his urgent need and focused on his fingers working her hard nub while he loosened his hold to allow her to move against his thigh, his jeans catching the ribbon far better than his bare thigh would have.

Lacey started to pant and her movements against him grew frantic until she squealed out her release.

Cole's heart warmed to have his only love fall apart in his arms and he brought her slowly back to earth while he counted to a hundred, trying to ignore his demanding cock. When he reached that high number and could feel Lacey relax, he removed his hand and licked at the juices on his fingers.

Wrong thing to do.

~~*~~

Lacey wasn't exactly sure how she'd gone from

sitting on Cole's lap, coming down from a very different orgasm than any she'd experienced, to kneeling before a hay bale.

"Bend over." Cole's voice was rough with need.

She loved that tone. The one that told her she could make him so hard he couldn't wait. It happened every time he brought her to orgasm first. Willingly, she bent over, but lifted up an inch as the scratchy hay brushed her sensitive nipples.

The sound of Cole's zipper opening behind her had her anticipation growing.

When his hands spread her ass cheeks, moving the butt plug just a hair, her body tightened all over again.

"Shit, Lacey. This looks amazing."

"It feels amazing too."

"Good. How does it feel with this?" Cole slid his large cock into her with one long thrust.

"Yesss." As her sheath expanded to accept him, he pushed against the plug in her ass and a wave of indescribable feeling flowed over her.

"Come with me." Cole's entreaty sent electricity flowing through her veins, but as he glided out of her and re-entered, everything started to spark.

His hands grasped her hips, keeping her cheeks spread. He had to be watching the butt plug and a thrill raced down her spine right to the center of her ass. Her sheath tightened around his cock as he exited her, his hands keeping her in place, only to pull her toward him as he pushed in again, his width stretching the ribbon on either side of her folds and pulling on the toy inside her.

Her muscles turned to mush as Cole's rhythm picked up speed and she couldn't hold herself away from the hay anymore. The scratching of it against the tips of her nipples as Cole pushed and pulled her back and forth brought squeals of delight she couldn't contain.

The multiple levels of stimulation overflowed her senses. Her entire body tensed and she released a scream of pleasure.

"Lacey!" Cole's shout echoed through her as her orgasm crested and his come filled her. Every nerve jumped for joy at their mutual ecstasy.

Cole's hands held her tight to his pelvis as he bucked a couple times with residual pleasure.

She looked back to find his eyes closed, his head tilted back slightly and his massive chest muscles tense. Her firefighting cowboy wasn't just over the top muscular, he had a heart of gold to go with it. Happiness floated through her. She was so thankful they had found each other again.

Cole opened his green eyes and smiled at her. "I love that I never know what I'll find beneath your clothes."

She shrugged. "You'll always find me."

He chuckled, and she dropped her head at the vibrations that hit her sensitive spots.

Cole pulled out of her, and she sucked in her breath as his glide hit the toy in her butt. She had doubted

Adriana, who told her how arousing it could be, but now she understood. She'd have to make the bartender a plate of her favorite cookies after this.

She knelt and quickly unhooked the corset, shivering as she removed the toy and set everything aside.

Cole took off his jeans and boots before pulling her back to lie against him on the soft sleeping bag. With one hand he covered them, and her quickly cooling body welcomed his warmth.

She laid her head on his shoulder and crossed one leg over his. "So I take it you liked that?"

His hand on her back held her against him. "I did. How about you?"

She nodded as she smiled up at him. "Definitely."

He squeezed her against him. "So should we keep this Christmas Eve gift-giving idea as our tradition?"

"I'd like to, but let's make it just one gift on Christmas Eve and the rest on Christmas day."

"That sounds good to me." He paused. "We won't have to spend every Christmas day at my parents. Maybe we could move around each Christmas, even having the family dinner in our new house when it's done."

Lacey stiffened. "As long as dinner at your parents' house is the last in the rotation."

"Lacey. We need to go to my parents' this year."

She leveraged herself up on her elbow to better look him in the eye. "No, we don't. I told you. I'm not spending Christmas dinner at your parents' ranch. They're the reason we lost eight years of being together…like this. I'm not ready to forgive them for that."

"They were just trying to do what was right for me."

"No, they weren't. They were doing what was best for them. They didn't care about you."

Cole tensed against her. "That's not true."

"Really?" Her stomach churned as it did every time she thought about what the Hatchers had done to their son. "Then why did they refuse to help you with your horse rescue ranch? Why did they tell Dillon he could have Sunrise Creek? Because they cared about you?"

"That's not fair, Lacey. They're my parents."

She couldn't contain her anger any longer. She sat up, pulling the sleeping bag with her. "Yes, they are and they should have put their child before their own selfish need to be important. Who's going to be at the party this year? The mayor? The governor? Or is it some millionaire who's looking for a horse?"

"I'm sure the town manager will be there, but that's not why we should go. It's the right thing to do. They're my parents."

She fisted her hands. Cole would always want to do what was right. "I think it's the wrong thing to do. I think they should suffer for a few years." She snorted. "That's assuming they would even notice you weren't there."

Cole sat up, too. "Thanks." His face was hard and her stomach clenched at the hurt in his eyes.

"That's not what I meant." She sighed and clasped

her hands over the sleeping bag. "Why can't we stay here? Everyone will be gone to your mother's. We could actually have some time alone, enjoy each other, maybe go for a ride."

Cole shook his head. "What are you going to do at our wedding? Or are you planning to wait eight years for us to marry?"

"No." She reached for his hand and grasped it, but he didn't hold hers in return. "I want to marry you. The sooner, the better. I just can't spend Christmas day with them. That's supposed to be a day of happiness and I'm bitter and angry at them for making you dump me all those years ago and for turning their backs on you when you wanted to start the horse rescue. It's only been two months since we found each other again. I just need some time to come to terms with what they did."

Cole looked away. "Time away from them isn't going to help. Only if you are around them will you be able to see they aren't monsters."

"Or they may prove they're even worse than I thought."

His gaze came back to hers, his brows furrowed with hurt. "I'm their son. If they are such monsters then I guess I'm not nearly good enough for you." He stood, pulling his hand from hers to grasp his jeans. "I'm going back in the house with *my family*."

"Cole."

He ignored her, stuffing his legs into his pants. "When

I get off my shift on Christmas morning, I'll come back here and see if you've changed your mind. If not, I'm going to my parents anyway." He grabbed up his boots and shirt and strode out of the barn.

Part of her wanted to go after him, but the other part was too angry to move. Couldn't he see that while he was raised to do what was right, his parents had no such compunction? They had treated him so poorly and yet he remained loyal, like an abused dog.

She didn't want to make it hard on him, but she just couldn't forgive them. Thanks to the rumors his mother spread, she and Cole lost eight years together. If she made him choose between them and her, he'd just shown her which way he would go. His parents would win again. Why couldn't he understand how she felt? Why did he have to push her so soon?

Shivering from both the cold temperature in the barn and her loss of Cole for the night, she snuggled between the sleeping bags. She wanted to go in, but if she did, he would see it as her agreeing to go, but if she went to his parents' house the chance that she'd make a terrible scene was very good and that would drive the wedge between them deeper. She hated that the Hatchers were once again tearing her and Cole apart.

She stared up at the snowflakes hanging from the rafters. Cole had given her such a thoughtful present and she'd ruined it. She looked around and noticed the bottle of wine for the first time. For some reason, that little gesture made her heart break. Tears filled her eyes, and she closed them against the ache in her chest.

25

Chapter Three

Cole woke at the sound of footsteps on the stairs. He glanced at the clock. It was three in the morning. Whoever climbed the stairs obviously didn't know where to step. He heard at least four of the stairs creak before his bedroom door opened.

He closed his eyes and waited. When the bed dipped, he silently sighed in relief. He had hoped she would come in before now, but at least she was inside. She pulled the covers over her, but didn't touch him.

He hated the hurt feeling in his stomach. Lacey was his world and usually they were on the same page about important stuff, but this thing with his parents was tearing him up.

The bed started to shimmy. What the…oh shit. She was shivering.

Anger resurfaced that the only reason she'd come in was to get warm, but he couldn't ignore his instinct to take care of her.

Rolling toward her, he threw his arm over her like he usually did in his sleep, pressing his chest against her chilled back and carefully keeping his hardening cock from touching her ass. When her cold hand grasped his forearm around her waist, relief that she still wanted his touch calmed him.

He didn't blame her for not wanting to spend Christmas day at his parents in Orson. Maybe he could keep the visit short, just a couple hours so they could start to see each other as relatives.

Then he and Lacey could stop by her parents, even though the Winters had told them they didn't have to, understanding Lacey's wish to spend her first Christmas with him. He admitted he wanted his parents to accept that as well, but since they hadn't, he was obligated to go.

He wasn't excited about visiting her parents either, but for a completely different reason. Guilt.

Lacey pressed her ass against his cock and his mind switched gears immediately, causing his cock to grow hard again. Her gift to him tonight had been very hot, her ass filled with the sex toy and pressing against him in her sheath. His cock hardened even more. Luckily, her even breathing made it clear she was asleep.

There was no way he would lose her. He had to find a way for her and his parents to at least get along. He could just imagine his wedding. His mom would whisper to her friends how disappointed she was that he had married "that little firebug" as she called Lacey, or she would predict the marriage wouldn't last. Lacey's fellow employees at Poker Flat Nudist Resort would close ranks around Lacey to defend her and would probably do everything in their power to shock his parents, friends, and relatives.

He had to figure out something. As he came up with one scenario after the other, discarding each in turn as unworkable, the minutes ticked by. In no time it was five in the morning and he had to get up and head over to the fire station. Reluctantly, he released Lacey and rose from the warm bed.

Though there was a chill in the air, he just threw on his sweatpants and headed for the bathroom. As he showered and shaved, his mind continued to focus on his problem. His father wasn't the issue. It was his mother. Dad just went along with what his mother wanted because it was easier that way.

He never understood his mother's drive to be important. His mom's sister, aunt Bonnie, was nothing like that. She was perfectly happy with her little shop in town, now that they had sold their ranch.

A knock on the door had Cole pausing as he dried off.

"Hey Cole, you almost done?"

"Yeah, Trace. I'll be right out." His cousin was another who had high hopes of acknowledgement and prosperity, only in his case they had crashed and burned with his divorce. Cole couldn't muster any resentment toward Trace. He'd learned the hard way.

Wrapping a towel about his waist, he grabbed up his sweatpants and opened the door. "All yours."

Trace stood there, his sun-streaked brown hair sticking up due to serious bedhead, in a white hotel bathrobe, probably from his days of homelessness until his wife froze his accounts and he was forced to move back in with aunt Bonnie. As far as Cole was concerned, his cousin was better off without the Ice Queen.

"Thanks." Trace closed the door and Cole moved down the hall to his room. Trace and Logan's predicaments made him even more appreciative of Lacey. He couldn't blame her for holding a grudge. After all, even he had thought her guilty of setting the fire. Now he just had to find a way to mend fences so he could keep both Lacey and his family.

Opening the door to his room, he was disappointed to find her gone. He'd hoped they could talk more calmly before he went to work. He glanced at the clock. Shit, he had to go. Quickly, he threw on his department t-shirt which was wrinkled from him throwing the clean clothes on the chair last night when he'd stormed in. He switched into an equally wrinkled pair of jeans then donned his boots. Grabbing up his cowboy hat on the way out of the room, he flew down the stairs and strode into the kitchen.

Coffee was ready, but his grandparents' door was still closed. That meant either Trace or Lacey had made it. He filled a travel mug then walked behind the stairs where the half-bath was located, now designated as Lacey's bathroom by his grandmother. The door was closed.

He wanted to say something, but finally gave up. Nothing he could say would keep them from another argument. He'd wait until tomorrow morning when he came home. He walked through the living room, completing his circle of the downstairs and headed outside.

"Have fun at work." Trace sat on a porch chair, sipping coffee.

His cousin's shiny new boots made Cole smile. "I will. At least I won't be mucking out Samson's and Lightyear's stalls."

Trace lost his grin. "Great. I expect you'll sleep through the night without a screaming baby in the next room, too."

"Only if the sound of the fire bell doesn't wake me, but this time of year, the chances of having a quiet night are about nil." He frowned as he jogged down the steps.

"Yeah, there is that. Good luck."

Cole raised his hand without looking back as he walked toward his truck. Once inside, he glanced back at the house. Trace had gone in and there was no sign of Lacey. He'd see her tomorrow morning. Hopefully, she'd be a little more willing to compromise.

He turned on the engine and backed his truck toward the house before heading down the driveway to the dirt road that would take him to Route 93.

It didn't take long to drive through the just waking town to the station. As he got out of his truck, Mason, the usual fire engine driver, pulled up. Cole waited for him to exit his SUV. "Morning Mason."

"Hey, Lieutenant. Heard you're pulling an extra-long shift today."

Cole nodded as he fell into step with Mason. "Just a couple extra hours. Giving Clark a little morning time with his kids on Christmas day. Then I'm off for four days, so I figured I could give up a couple hours."

Mason shook his head. "If I had a girlfriend as sweet looking as yours, I'd be hightailing it home as soon as I could." He slapped Cole on the back. "You're a better man then I am."

Cole gave the man a wan smile. He didn't feel like he was a better man. His argument with Lacey sat like a wet firehose in his stomach. He had the next twenty-four hours to figure out what to do. Mason was right. He had something special and he needed to do whatever it took to hold on to it while still doing what was right.

~~*~~

Lacey held her cup of coffee as she stared out the large living room window framed by garland, the lights not twinkling as they were unplugged during the day. She hadn't said goodbye to Cole, too much of a coward to come out when she heard his distinctive stride descending the stairs. Now she wished she had. What if he got hurt? Or worse? She always worried while he was at work, but today it was doubled.

"Hey, Blondie, why the sad face? He'll be home tomorrow."

She didn't even try to smile. "I know, Trace, but every shift means he's putting himself in danger. I can't help but worry he could get hurt. He even admitted that this time of year has an increase in house fires. I wish they would outlaw live Christmas trees. Then he'd be safer and less people would lose their homes."

Trace put his arm over her shoulders. "I agree with you, but I think trying to get that law passed here in Arizona would be as difficult as finding gold in the ranch's old copper mine. Just not going to happen."

She patted his hand. "I know. But a girl has to have a dream."

He chuckled at that. "I thought that monstrous ranch house you're building on Fire Hill was your dream."

She smiled. "First of all, it's not that big and second of all, who said I was limited to one dream?"

Trace stepped away and held up his hands. "No one. Last I heard there's no limit on dreams. I certainly hope not. Just when all mine came true, I lost them." He headed for the front door. "Now I get to muck out Samson's and Lightyear's stalls. Hope I remember how. Last time I did this I was sixteen years old."

This time she smiled and winked. "It's like riding a bike, you never forget how. You don't forget the smell either."

"Thanks." He gave her a pained look before he opened the front door and headed for the barn.

She didn't envy him his task. As the latest family member to arrive at Last Chance Ranch, Trace was assigned the worst chores, but it was expected. Cowboys accepted that they had to pay their dues. Trace would do a great job. He always made sure every corner of the barn was—oh no!

She set her coffee cup down on the coffee table and ran out the door after Cole's cousin. When she got to the barn, Trace was standing at the entrance to the last stall where she and Cole had started their Christmas Eve tradition.

He turned as she ran up, frantically trying to remember if the corset could be seen from where he was standing. When she reached him, he turned toward her, his eyebrow raised. "I take it this is yours and Cole's doing?"

Her cheeks heated. "We just wanted a little alone time last night."

"Smart idea. I might just try it myself. Your friend Billy tends to snore. He's not that loud, but sometimes he sounds like a burro."

She moved slowly into the stall. "Just think when our house is finished, you can have our room."

"Yeah. That's one thing I can look forward to." Something in his voice had her stopping.

"You okay?"

He shrugged. "Sure. Do you want me to pick this up for you?"

He was definitely not happy, a regular state for him after losing the woman he loved, his ranch and his substantial bank account all at once. There wasn't anything she could do to help him with that. Cole said Trace needed time. "No, I'll clean it up. Then I'll take Angel out into the corral so she will be more comfortable while you work in here."

Trace shook his head. "The man that abused her should get the electric chair. To mar such a beauty should be punishable by death."

Lacey silently agreed. "He's awaiting trial, but don't worry. Cole will be testifying along with the vet who treated her when she first came here. I'm counting on him going to jail."

Trace turned and headed for the tack room. "I hope they throw the book at him."

As soon as he was out of sight, she searched behind the hay bale and found the corset and sex toy. She quickly wrapped them in one of the sleeping bags. Then she zipped up the other sleeping bag and rolled it up. Two trips to the house later, she had put everything away, setting the bottle of wine in their room. She was more determined than ever for her and Cole to stay on the ranch tomorrow. They needed some serious time alone and not just for sex.

Missing the rest of her caffeine for the morning, she headed downstairs and picked up her coffee cup. When she entered the large eat-in kitchen, she found Logan half asleep in a chair and Cole's grandmother, Annette, cooing to the baby as she fed her. For such a tiny girl, six-month-old Charlotte had the whole house jumping to her tune. "Good morning. Is there any coffee left?"

Annette nodded without taking her eyes off Charlotte. "There sure is. I just made a new pot for sleepyhead over here."

Logan scowled at his grandmother. "I'd like to see how chipper you'd be if I put Charlotte in your room for a night."

Lacey couldn't help her lip quirking upward. Cole's oldest cousin and most confirmed bachelor was not taking to fatherhood very well. It didn't help that there was no mother in sight. "I'm sure she'll start sleeping the night soon, won't she, Annette?"

Annette wiped a bit of baby food off Charlotte's lips before replying. "Of course she will, right, sweetie? You'll sleep through the night eventually, when you're good and ready."

Logan's scowl darkened and Lacey's heart went out to him. She wanted children, but not for years yet. She couldn't imagine having one now, never mind being a single parent. Then again he should have expected it to happen eventually. He had the striking features of his mother's side of the family, a sharp jaw and dark eyes with wrinkle lines in the corners from squinting in the Arizona sun. Add to that his short ponytail of sun-streaked brown hair and lack of inclination to smile just made him that much more of a challenge to the cowgirls.

"There's some homemade cinnamon buns I made last night in the refrigerator, Lacey." Annette spoke, but didn't take her eyes off the baby. "If you're looking for breakfast, they warm up in the microwave pretty well."

"They're very good." Logan's comment surprised her. He wasn't one to offer praise often.

She'd had Annette's cinnamon buns before and she didn't need any extra encouragement. "That sounds perfect. Anyone else want one warmed up while I'm at it?"

"I ate, honey, didn't I, Charlotte?" Annette didn't let the baby answer. Instead she got another spoonful of food into Charlotte's mouth. She was totally enraptured with her great-granddaughter, which was one of the reasons Logan had come to Last Chance Ranch. The man clearly needed help raising his child.

"I'll take one, if you don't mind." He looked longingly at the pan she pulled from the fridge.

"Logan Williams, you already had two." Annette's voice was stern, even if she didn't spare a glance for her grandson.

Lacey looked over her shoulder at him and saw his hopeful expression dissolve into a frown. Poor man. Taking out a bun, she put it on a plate and set it in the microwave. He needed all the food he could get in order to handle his work on the ranch *and* taking care of Charlotte when his grandmother tired.

When the microwave dinged, she took out a second

bun and put it in the microwave. She really did like Cole's family. In a way, she wished his mother had been adopted, but since she had the exact same chestnut colored hair Annette used to have and most of her facial features, there was little chance of that. Where had her future mother-in-law picked up her high-end ambitious streak?

The microwave dinged again and she took the two plates to the table and set one down in front of Logan before grabbing her coffee and sitting down with her own.

"You're an angel, you know that?" He took a bite of the warm, sugary bun.

She chuckled. "Can't say anyone has ever called me that. If you want a real Angel, there's one in the corral right now."

Logan looked at her strangely before understanding dawned. "I'm glad that horse will let you near her. She looks at me like I'm the devil or something."

She couldn't respond because her tongue was enraptured by the heavy cinnamon treat in her mouth. After swallowing, she sighed. "It's not you. It's just men in general and I think the bigger you are, the more afraid she is. Cole had to drug her just to treat her. I'm so glad he uses a female vet or I think Angel would have died."

Annette stood to put the spoon and bowl she'd used for the baby into the sink. "Cole's a good man. Every horse he's brought here has needed this place. Now with more help," she paused to look at Logan, "we can take more horses."

"Thanks to you and Ed." Lacey smiled at Cole's grandmother, but the woman waved it off.

"We just had a place that wasn't being used anyway. He's done the bulk of the work." She unstrapped Charlotte from the highchair and picked her up. "Now I'm going to go play with my beautiful great-grandbaby because her daddy needs to fix the arm of the porch chair in the far corner like he's been promising Cole for the last two months."

"Grandma, it's Christmas Eve."

"That's right and it would make a nice present for your cousin when he gets home from the fire station tomorrow morning. Now go. You have plenty of time before we have to leave for your mother's house."

Logan unfolded his tall body from the chair and shuffled out of the room. It wasn't that he was lazy, he was just in a perpetually bad mood. Then again, no sleep would do that to a person.

Annette turned toward Lacey. "Are you sure you're okay being alone here overnight? We won't see you until the big dinner party tomorrow evening. Are you sure you don't want to come with us today?"

Lacey didn't want to insult Annette by telling her how much she was looking forward to the peace and quiet. "I'll be fine. I have a few projects I plan to work on and I want to be here when Cole comes home tomorrow."

"Okay, honey. Would you mind throwing the rest of the dishes in the dishwasher for me?"

She smiled. "I'd be happy to." When Annette asked someone to do something, there was only one answer. Yes.

"Thank you." She nuzzled Charlotte as she walked from the room. "Are you ready to play dress up with granny?"

Lacey popped the last bite of cinnamon bun into her mouth and chewed slowly. She'd been an only child and the busyness of Last Chance was sometimes overwhelming, but now, when it suddenly went quiet, it made her wonder what it would be like for her and Cole in their new house.

Standing, she picked up her plate. The privacy would definitely be welcome as would the quiet. But maybe they could start another tradition, one where his family came over for Sunday dinner.

She rinsed her plate and added it to the dishwasher along with the few dishes and cups in the sink. As soon as she finished her chore, she would wrap the last presents she had bought for Cole.

An uneasy feeling crawled up her spine. She hated not kissing him goodbye and telling him she loved him. Crossing her fingers, she pushed the button on the dishwasher and it whirred to life. *Please, let there be no fires today.*

Chapter Four

Tired, Cole dropped into his bunk at the firehouse. Two fires in one day and it was only nine o'clock. That had to be some kind of record. The last house had tugged hard on his heart. The little blonde girl with her braid over one shoulder and a stuffed bunny in her arms reminded him too much of Lacey. His fiancée may have been a teenager when her parents' carriage house caught fire, but like the little girl, she'd been inside and had to escape through flames.

The little girl at the fire was heartbroken because Santa wouldn't know where to find her tonight. Lacey had been heartbroken because he broke up with her. That guilt just piled on top of the guilt he already had. Lacey said it was his mother's fault he dumped her, but if he had really loved her, he would have rebelled. He hadn't been smart enough to know what he had back then. He was smart enough now.

So why wasn't he telling his mother to take her Christmas party and shove it?

Because she was his mother.

He couldn't get around that fact. He'd been brought up to respect his parents and be loyal to family. That meant when his mother asked him specifically to be at Sunrise Creek Ranch for Christmas dinner, he needed to go, especially after he and Lacey had spent Thanksgiving at Last Chance.

The sound of the alert tone had Cole throwing off the blankets and running to the pole. Once down in the locker room, he stuffed his legs into his turnout pants as he listened to the particulars coming in from dispatch.

"Fuck! What a Christmas season this is turning out to be." Mason grabbed his coat and ran for the truck.

Cole was right behind him. "It's another house fire. Shit, I hope they all got out." As the fourth man jumped on the engine, Mason pulled the truck out of the garage and onto Copper Win Road.

Less than four minutes later they pulled into the neighborhood and could see flames licking up the side of an old house. This area of town was referred to as the "old" section even though homes didn't date back more than fifty years. Still, that meant none probably met present day fire codes. Mason stopped the engine and one man jumped out and secured the hose to a hydrant. Cole waited for the signal then turned to Mason. "Go."

The truck rolled to a stop, three houses up the street. A woman with two children stood at the end of the driveway. He strode toward her. "Is anyone still inside?"

"No. It's just me and my two children. I just ran to the store for milk. I wasn't gone more than thirty minutes."

Cole's heart slowed now that he had confirmation no one's life was in danger. He spoke into his radio. "No one's inside. Let's knock this baby down and see if we can't save Christmas." After ordering another man to use the two and a half inch hose, Cole strode to the police unit that pulled up.

"Better evacuate the nearby houses in case the wind shifts. Just a precautionary measure. These houses are old." The officer nodded and he and his partner took over crowd control.

Cole moved back to the woman with the two children.

The little girl in her mother's arms was clearly scared. The poor kid.

"Mr. Fireman, can I get in the firetruck?"

He turned his attention to the boy whose eyes were filled with excitement. He probably would have reacted the same way at his age. "Not tonight, son. But your mom can bring you over to the station any time after Christmas and we'll be glad to give you a tour."

The boy frowned before leaning into his mom's hip.

"Ma'am, do you have any idea how this fire started?"

She shook her head.

"Do you happen to have a live Christmas tree?"

"No. I can't afford that. I couldn't even afford to buy more propane when we ran out last week. I was waiting until I got paid on Thursday."

Standing in the street in a pair of jeans and a sweatshirt, her children in their pajamas and winter coats, she looked like any other family in the neighborhood who stood gawking as his men worked to put out the fire.

A growing concern for his men forced him to delve deeper. The reason for the fire was Detective Anderson's job, but Cole's men could be walking into a potentially hazardous situation. "Ma'am, what kind of heat do you have?"

"Propane." She scowled. "It's also what I cook with. I've been using the propane in the grill to heat water."

Cole's gut tightened at the thought of what she may have done. "What did you do to stay warm?"

"I used an old electric heater I have. It only warmed the living room, but that's where we've been having a camp out." She looked down at her son before raising her brows, signaling the need to put a positive spin on it.

Cole couldn't stop his groan, but thanks to the noise of the fire and water, she didn't appear to hear. "So you all had sleeping bags on the floor?"

She brushed the hair away from her daughter's face. "Yes. It was a tight fit, but that's what it would be like in a tent. I used my father's old sleeping bag from when he used to go fishing and my kids had the ones their grandmother bought them a couple years ago."

He'd bet his next paycheck the mother's sleeping bag, the oldest and least flame retardant, had been pushed against the heater which started the fire. In a way he was relieved. At least they had a chance of saving the building and didn't have to worry about propane fuel or a kerosene heater, which had been his concern.

One of his men called over the radio. "We have it under control."

Cole took a breath. "Good. It appears it may have been caused by an electric heater."

"Seriously?"

He grimaced as the firefighter's voice game over the radio loud enough for the woman to hear.

He directed his man. "Soak it down good. We don't want any embers floating to the houses next door."

"Got it, Lieutenant."

The young mother looked embarrassed as he turned back to her.

"I was just trying to keep my kids warm. No one here knows I'm out of propane." She grabbed his arm. "You won't tell them, will you? I mean, I don't want them to know how tight money has been for me."

Though many emotions barreled through him at the mother's plea, disbelief overrode them all and he had no idea why. It was completely irrational. Pushing aside his strange irritation, he tapped into his sympathy for her plight. "Ma'am, don't worry. I won't be talking to your neighbors. We all experience financial difficulties at one time or another." He certainly had before Lacey took over his finances. "I'm sure, like me, your neighbors will be happy that you and your children are alive and unharmed."

The woman glanced at the crowd being kept away for safety's sake before meeting his gaze, her own uncertain.

"Why don't you take your children back there where you all will be safe, and I will see what I can do to get this fire out completely."

She nodded and turned, but then looked back at him. "Thank you." He nodded once, and she walked into the crowd of neighbors, all anxious to hear from her what happened.

Once she'd left, his irritation returned. He shouldn't be so bothered by the woman's concern about what her neighbors thought, but it was like a blister that had finally started bleeding. He strode back to the engine and Mason. "How's the pressure?"

The man gave him a searching look. "Fine, why wouldn't it be?"

He shrugged carelessly as he looked at the small house, not really seeing it. "Just tired of tragedies at Christmas."

"I don't think this one will be a tragedy. Everyone is alive and at least half the building will be saved. We do have a pretty good reputation around here for putting out fires."

Cole snapped his head around to look at Mason and found the man smiling.

"Yeah, you're right. We do good work." He walked away to look at the scene from the side, away from everyone. His irritation at the single mother still bothered him. The poor woman just lost part of her home and was barely making ends meet with two kids. Who was he to judge her? Gossip running rampant in a neighborhood could ruin it for a person living there. He of all people knew that. It's what originally drove Lacey from Orson.

So why did he take the woman's comment to heart?

He started back toward the engine. It was probably just all the calls in one shift. They usually got about two a week. He was spoiled.

The fire took little time to extinguish. He handed the woman the paperwork and asked her to bring it down to the station in the next couple days. It was Christmas Eve and she had more pressing problems than finding her insurance company name and number, if she even had insurance. Still, it was almost midnight before they rolled into the station again.

Some of the men headed straight for the kitchen. No surprise as once the adrenaline rush had worn off, they were starving, but he just wanted to get some sleep. Hanging up his gear, he trudged upstairs to his bunk and lay down.

Relaxing into the bed, he focused on Lacey, her bright smile, golden hair, mahogany-colored eyes. His heart swelled that this woman was his and he finally drifted off to sleep.

The sound of the alert tone woke him again. He glanced at the clock. 3:00 a.m. What the fuck?

~~*~~

The sound of a quail near the house woke Lacey. She glanced at the clock. It was already after seven. Cole would be home at noon. Her heartbeat sped at the thought, but her stomach tensed.

It was Christmas day.

She wanted to believe they would have a wonderful day alone, unwrapping the presents downstairs and eating the dinner she'd had Selma, the cook at Poker Flat, make for her as a surprise for Cole. It was in the refrigerator waiting for his decision. She'd even bought peppermint stick ice cream for dessert. It actually had pieces of candy cane in it, Cole's favorite Christmas candy.

She threw the covers off and sat up. If only she could be sure she could convince him to stay. If not, she might very well be spending the day alone.

She stood then headed for the bathroom. No way. If he had to go to his parents because it was "the right thing to do," then she'd drive over to Poker Flat and hang out with Adriana and Billy and anyone else who was there. But in the meantime, she would hope for the best and prepare to welcome Cole home for Christmas.

After showering, she pulled out the special lingerie she'd bought just for Christmas Day. It was a red body stocking with a few delicate green bows that hid nothing. It wasn't the typical mesh that Cole had seen her wear in a bra on occasion. This body stocking had spaghetti straps so the neckline revealed her cleavage, but then there was a strip of see-through red nylon over her nipples. Below that, large holes between three and five inches in diameter were cut out so a lot of her skin showed, including the bottom of her breasts, but all her critical areas were covered, except that pulling a cut-out to a strategic place was very easy with the stretchy nylon.

What she liked most about it was it was comfortable, yet it gave her a soft stimulation when she had no clothes on. She loved wearing sexy lingerie under her clothes on a daily basis. She was always excited to see what Cole thought of it at night, plus during the day, she smiled often as she thought about what she had on, which no one guessed at.

Throwing on a pair of jeans, a red sweater since it was Christmas and her brown cowboy boots, she jogged down the stairs to find breakfast. As she ate a leftover cinnamon bun and drank her coffee, the lack of noise started to bother her. How odd? She always wished for a quiet morning like this and now that she had one, it felt strange.

She shrugged. She'd just become use to all the activity since Billy and the cousins had joined them. She looked forward to sitting at the breakfast table with just Cole, chatting about what they would do for the day.

And if Cole was at work? She could always come back to the Williams house and have coffee with Annette… except Annette would be totally involved with little Charlotte. Hmmm. She could go into work early on the days Cole worked then she wouldn't notice being alone.

Standing, she picked up her plate and after rinsing

it, put it in the dishwasher. Feeding the horses wasn't her usual chore, but since no one else was home, she was more than happy to do so. Grabbing her jean jacket off the hook by the door, she stuffed her arms into the sleeves and stepped outside.

She breathed deeply before walking down the steps to the porch toward the barn. The sun was shining and she left her jacket unbuttoned, the day already warming up. Once inside, she grabbed the pitchfork and dug into the loose hay Logan had piled up for her the day before.

She could certainly lift a bale of hay, even if she was small, but Cole and his cousins were quick to help her. Still, it caught her off guard when surly Logan would go the extra mile for her, or Trace, who had no use for women after the fiasco with his wife, actually gave her a reassuring squeeze like he had the day before. She could only chalk it up to being part of the family. A warmth filled her chest at the thought. She liked being part of the mish-mash family on Last Chance. As an only child, she just wasn't use to all the activity.

After pitching hay into Lightyear's stall, she moved on to the next one where Tiny Dancer awkwardly stood at her approach. Each horse had its own unique personality and she loved them all, but hopefully they would all find forever families.

After feeding the rest of the horses, she moved to Angel's stall. "Hey, sweetie. Ready for breakfast?" She pitched in the hay.

The scarred white Arabian walked toward her, ignoring the food and instead stuck her head over the stall door.

"Good morning to you too, Angel." Lacey looped her arm around the mare's neck and pressed her cheek to the horse's cheek. "Would you like to go for a ride a little later? Maybe check on the new house?" She moved her head away and stroked the horse before giving her a couple pats and stepping back.

Angel stepped back and finally lowered her head to eat.

Lacey returned the pitchfork to its hook on the wall and headed back to the house. A ride out to the construction site would make her feel a lot better about her future and would waste some time until Cole got home.

The sun had increased the temperature already, so she left her coat on the peg by the front door and went into the kitchen to grab a few jelly beans, Angel's favorite treat, and a granola bar for herself in case she got hungry. Pulling a water bottle from the fridge, she had her hand on the door when she remembered Cole's rule. If she ever went riding by herself, she had to bring a gun with her. He said there were too many dangers in the desert and most of the acres of Last Chance Ranch had no cell service, an issue they would have to tackle at their new house.

She stepped around the corner to the gun case. All the men had their own guns, but Cole had shown her how to use his 12-gauge shotgun. She liked it because her aim didn't have to be perfect, and it wasn't.

After taking it out and pocketing a few shells, she closed the case and headed outside to the barn.

The last thing she needed to do before taking Angel out was to move Samson and Lightyear into the corral. She set her water, snack and the gun in the empty stall she and Cole had made love in, then strode to the tack room and pulled a halter off the wall. Luckily, Samson had learned to tolerate her over the last couple months since she started coming to Last Chance, and he didn't give her any trouble as she looped the halter over his head and led him to the corral. Once he was safely closed in, she moved to Lightyear's stall, but she couldn't open the stall door. "Really?"

She stared at the 4-wheeler blocking the door. If Billy were the one who left it parked there, he would be mucking out Angel's stall when he got back from Poker Flat. The keys were still in it, but she didn't want to startle Angel, so she disengaged the brake and pushed the machine a couple feet until it was out of the way.

Rolling her shoulders and taking a few deep breaths, she opened the stall door. Trace had already put the halter on Lightyear since the horse hated anyone touching his face. Luckily, he tolerated a halter or bridle well and she led Lightyear out into the corral. Gingerly, she released him from the halter and he shook his head as if the one minute walk from barn to corral had been an eternity.

Striding back into the barn, she found Angel waiting

for her. She chuckled. "Hmm, I guess someone is anxious to go for a run."

The horse eyed her, watching her every move as she went into the tack room and brought out a bridle. She wasn't the best horsewoman, but Angel was a good girl for her when they rode.

She struggled with the weight of the saddle as usual, but the wood steps Cole set up for her to help her throw it onto the horse's back worked perfectly. Maybe she should think about exercising with weights.

Once she had the saddle secured and double checked, she stuffed her snack and Angel's treat into the saddlebag and secured the gun. She brought Angel out of her stall and using one of the steps again, she mounted, walking them outside into the bright day.

Lacey kicked Angel into a canter down the long road to the construction that would soon be her new house. There wasn't a cloud in the sky and the cool temperature had disappeared. She'd bet it was already over sixty degrees. The land was still and quiet with no breezes blowing and just a couple large birds catching the thermals far overhead.

She loved the varied browns of the desert dotted with the green of the saguaro cacti and the scrawny mesquite trees. They'd had to clear most of the mesquite from the top of the Fire Hill where the house was being built, but there had been no saguaros up there so they hadn't needed to relocate them.

Within fifteen minutes, she slowed Angel and they

walked up the hill to the construction site. Cole was right. They did need a barn here. At least for horses that needed his care around the clock. Then she could keep Angel nearby. Everyone living on the ranch understood Angel's fear, but the men often forgot that just being in the barn working caused her a lot of stress.

Lacey leaned down and patted Angel. "I'm going to take care of you, sweetie. You're just plain stuck with me." She sat up again and guided her horse around the construction site. There were some walls up, and pipes sticking up from the poured slab, but there was still so much to do. She looked forward to the day when she and Cole could make love in their own house…anywhere in the house.

She smiled. She'd have to insist on a sturdy kitchen table.

As she and Angel came around the end of the house, she heard a hum in the distance. Shading her eyes against the morning sun, she could see dust billowing along the road. It was the ATV.

Chapter Five

Her heart jumped at the sight. It had to be Cole. She looked at her watch, but it was only quarter after nine. Maybe the man he was covering for this morning finished opening presents with his children early. She nudged Angel into a walk down the hill. She'd like to gallop up and meet him, but that would put added stress on Angel. She didn't like the ATV and she only tolerated Cole.

As the vehicle approached, she squinted to see her fiancé, but it wasn't him. Of course it wasn't. Cole would ride Samson.

Dread formed in the pit of her stomach. Was it another firefighter come to tell her Cole had been injured? She gripped the reigns at the thought. Angel stood completely still waiting with her.

Finally, she was able to make out the face of the man driving the ATV and she didn't recognize him from the fire station. Nor was he one of the family she'd met. He had dark, bushy eyebrows and a white, unkempt beard. His shoulders looked to be in a permanent hunch, but she couldn't be sure because his shirt and vest hung off him like they were far too big.

The man pointed at her and yelled across the distance still between them. "Give me that horse!"

No sooner did she understand his words than Angel bolted. Lacey grasped the pommel to stay on as the horse raced away farther from the main house and the man determined to catch them.

Lacey's heart beat as fast as a rattlesnake's rattle as the implications of her predicament became clear. The man had to be Angel's former owner, Ray Norton, the one that had beat her within inches of her life.

Fear and anger tore through Lacey. He'd obviously expected everyone to be gone for Christmas and planned to steal Angel back. She wouldn't let that happen.

She let Angel go where she felt safest. That was northwest of the house and into an area Lacey had never been. She glanced back to see Ray still after them.

The horse turned and started up an incline of a canyon. The shale slipped out from beneath Angel's hooves and Lacey held tight, her breathing now as erratic as her horse's.

"Come on girl, you can do it."

Angel seemed to take heart at her words and battled through the loose rock until they made surer ground. As they rose, smaller rocks gave way to large boulders and stone formations carved by the wind. Finally, Angel slowed near the top of the canyon wall and Lacey guided her behind a long row of tall boulders, where she halted.

Once she was behind the natural monoliths, she checked to be sure she was hidden from Ray's view. From Angel's back, she could see over a five foot incline where there was a plateau of nothing but sagebrush and Joshua trees. If she headed up, maneuvering around the trees would make slow going and the man would easily see her and Angel unless they had a larger head start.

Lacey slid off her horse and pulled the gun from the saddle. She hugged Angel and pet her, pretending a calmness she didn't feel. "Stay right here, girl," she whispered. More than a little nervous, she crept up to a spot between two large boulders to look through a crack between them.

The sight was a little reassuring. The ATV spun out on the shale at the bottom of the hill, making no headway at all. She could hear the man swearing even over the sound of the engine.

Her body lost some of its tenseness. If the ATV couldn't make it up the canyon wall, then they were safe. She could take Angel onto the plateau and try to find a way home. Moving back to the horse, she gave her another hug. "It's okay, girl. We'll be safe soon."

Her last word sounded loud and she listened to the suddenly quiet canyon. Had he turned around and left?

Creeping back to the crack, she peered down below. What was he doing?

The man had turned the ATV back down to solid ground and turned off the engine. He jumped off and reached behind his back. When his hand came out from behind him, the sun glinted off the metal of a handgun.

"Oh crap."

Angel huffed behind her.

"It's okay, girl." She reached into her pocket and grabbed a shotgun shell. As much as she'd like to kill the man, she wasn't sure she had it in her. She hadn't even shot a snake yet.

Loading the gun with the shell, she had just reached into her pocket for another when his voice travelled up the canyon.

"Get your prissy ass out here, you worthless nag!" A shot rang out and Lacey dropped to the ground.

Angel reared, tearing the reins from the rock they'd been looped around.

"Angel, no!" Lacey scrambled up to grab at the reins, but her horse was too fast. Within seconds, Angel had raced up the last five feet of hill and disappeared over the rim, just as another shot rang out, hitting the dirt above Lacey's head, which sent tiny pebbles ricocheting everywhere. "Ow!"

Despite her dive for the ground, a pebble hit her arm, digging in so hard, it took her sweater with it.

"Fuckin' horse!" Ray's anger was bone chilling.

She ignored the pain in her arm, the need to see compelling her forward as she crawled to the crack again only to see Angels' former owner trying to hike up the shale base of the incline.

He slipped and fell at least three times before he finally found a handhold that brought his feet to more solid ground.

Sugar, in minutes, he would be up the canyon wall and after Angel. Despite the hammering of her heart, she steadied her shaking hands and lifted the shotgun just above the crack in the rock and aimed for a spot over the head of the ascending man. Squeezing her eyes shut, she pulled the trigger.

~~*~~

Whisper Adams rubbed her eyes, certain she hadn't seen what she thought she saw. Nope, she was still seeing a white horse with an empty saddle walking among the Joshua trees. This required investigating immediately.

After wiping her Uncle's mouth with a Christmas napkin, she set the bowl of oatmeal down. "I'll be right back, Joey."

The man's eyes implored her to be careful. He'd heard the muffled gunshots as well.

"Don't worry. I'll take Sal with me."

Grabbing her Glock 42, she stuck Sal into the waistband of her jeans and opened the trailer door.

"Well, strip me naked and throw me in a lava pit."

The white horse was still there, pawing at the dirt and walking in circles like it was lost. But horses didn't get lost. They always knew their way home, their way back for food. Something was seriously wrong.

Whisper walked slowly toward the agitated animal who meandered among the Joshua trees just outside the circle of her front yard. When its gaze rested on her, she stopped and held out her hand as if she would shake hands. Keeping her gaze on the horse's eye, she slowly turned her palm toward the desert floor and lowered her hand forty-five degrees.

The horse's nostrils flared but it didn't move away. That was something.

Without taking her eyes from the horse, she bent her knees and knelt on the ground.

The horse's head lowered, but it still didn't move.

Okay, she could be patient. She lowered her hand until her palm was flat on the desert floor in front of her.

Finally, the horse walked toward her.

She remained still as it sniffed her hair and clothes. When it stopped, she carefully stood up and lifted her palm to the horse's neck, never once breaking eye contact. But when her hand rubbed over rippled skin, she moved her gaze and froze.

This horse had been abused. Rage burned in her stomach and she removed her hand to avoid communicating her emotion to the horse. Bile rose in her throat and she turned away as her body trembled. She clenched her hands in an attempt to keep from vomiting, but it was no use.

She leaned over as her breakfast came up, spilling to the hard packed earth. It didn't take long to empty her pissed-off stomach. When there was nothing left, she wiped her mouth with her sleeve and turned to find the horse watching her. She grinned sheepishly. "Just a little weakness of mine."

Now that she'd gotten that out of the way, she ran her hand over the horse, not hesitating as it passed over brutal scars that conjured up beatings with chains and nasty whips. As she walked on the other side, she found the marks to be less. For the scars to have healed meant the horse was no longer around the person who had abused it. For that she was thankful.

"I'm going to call you Sacnite. That means white flower in one of the Native American languages. Don't ask me which one. I think maybe Mayan. I get them mixed up. Never was good at quizzes. They're a waste of time if you ask me."

She finished her inspection. "I don't know who would abuse such a beautiful mare. You're safe now, but you're awfully sweaty. I bet you're thirsty, too."

She picked up the reins and led the horse toward the trailer then dropped them. "Wait here and I'll get you some water."

Turning her back on Sacnite, she unburied an empty plaster bucket from the shed she'd built and brought it to the side of the trailer. She had to go into town tomorrow anyway to refill their water, so she wasn't worried about giving the horse what was left. Even if that weren't the case, she'd rather go without water than make an animal give it up.

After filling the bucket full from the spigot on the trailer, she brought it to Sacnite.

The horse lowered its head and drank.

Now she'd have to see what she could find for food. She had some hay leftover from last week when Motley left. Damn burro didn't even say thank you.

Moving around the trailer to where a palo verde tree leaned against a boulder that provided some protection from the sun at certain times of the day, she picked up an armful of the hay Motley left and brought it to where Sacnite drank.

The horse lifted its head from the water and shuffled the hay around a bit before deciding it was good enough to eat.

Seriously? This horse must be used to fresher hay. Reluctantly, her gaze shifted to the well-worn, but obviously expensive saddle. Ignoring the implications, she walked into the trailer to report to her uncle. He may not be able to move or talk beyond a grunt or groan, but his hearing was still good.

When she entered the cool interior, his gaze swung to her.

"It's a white mare that has been abused. She must

have run for a while. I gave her some of the hay from last week's visitor."

Uncle Joey nodded jerkily to show he understood, but then he raised his right eyebrow, the one that didn't sag.

She plopped down in the chair opposite him, careful not to hit the three foot Christmas tree with her elbow. "You want to know about the gunshots."

He nodded again.

She looked away. "Probably just some hunters out looking for quail or deer. It's snowbird season. All kinds of tourists come to Arizona to do crazy stuff."

A grunt issued from Joey's slack mouth.

She refused to look at him, well aware he didn't buy her explanation for a minute. He wanted her to investigate further. For an eighty-three-year-old man who'd had three strokes, he could be downright pushy. Of course if she were in his position, she'd be worried about what someone might do to her as well.

She finally looked at him. "Alright already. I'll go find out what happened. Happy?"

Joey's mouth opened, the closest he could get to a smile.

She stood, throwing her hand to the side in dismissal. "You're a taskmaster Uncle Joey. I should call Social Services on you."

She grabbed her brown cowboy hat that had seen better days and plopped it on her head. About to open the trailer door, she stilled. If someone was hurt or dying out there, she may need more than her gun.

Pushing aside the silver and gold garland, she pulled her canvass shoulder bag from the hook near the door, she stuck her arm through it and on further thought, grabbed up her rifle as well.

"I'll be back in a couple hours at most. You eat enough for me to be gone that long?"

Joey nodded again, his eyes watching her every move.

"Okay." She pointed to the clock across from him. "Noontime at the latest." After getting a look of understanding in the man's eyes, she opened the door and headed out.

~~*~~

"Fucking bitch!" The sound of sliding rock accompanied the swearing.

Lacey released a relieved sigh before opening her eyes to see what happened. There was a big hole not three feet away from where the man had been standing. Her hands started to shake again at how close she'd come to killing him. He was nowhere to be seen, but she'd bet a carton of Cole's favorite orange popsicles he had scurried behind the large red boulder not far from the hole she'd made. And she'd bet a plate of Selma's churros that the man was hurting too, if not from shotgun shot then from the rocks she'd hit.

At the thought of rocks, her arm drew her attention.

It still stung, but it would probably bleed profusely if she pulled her sweater and dislodged the stone. The idea had her brow sweating. Maybe if she was careful with her movements, she could just leave it alone until she got home.

Tears sprang to her eyes. How the heck was she supposed to get home with Ray shooting below her and no horse to ride on? She was miles from the main house now. She looked up to the rim, but didn't see any sign of Angel. If she crawled high enough to see, she'd be an easy target, especially for a madman who tried to get back a horse he'd beaten by shooting at it.

Determination rose. There was no way she'd let that man anywhere near Angel again. If she had to shoot him, so be it. Reaching into her pocket, she brought out the shells she had left. Only two. She wasn't exactly a good shot as proven by the hole three feet away from where Ray had stood when she'd actually been aiming for over his head.

"God damn, mother fucking, cock sucking stinking bitch." The grumbling coming from below had her blushing. Even Cole and his cousins didn't swear that much. Then again, they knew she'd been raised not to swear at all.

"Ow! Fuck. Fucking cunt! If I wanted to bleed to death, I would have got me a bronco." A stone flew out from behind the boulder.

At least she had confirmation of where he hid. She

looked down at her watch. It was almost ten. What if she couldn't get back before noon, when Cole was supposed to come home? Would he think she hid from him on purpose because she didn't want to go to his parents' house? Right now she wished she was at his parents'. It would be a crap load safer.

More grumbling came from behind the rock, none of it reassuring. The man was pissed.

She glanced up at the rim, hoping Angel didn't come back to find her. She had no doubt the man below would kill her horse the second he saw it.

"Hey gal." The voice from behind the rock was sickly sweet. "I just want my horse back. What do you say you let me get up this canyon wall and find it? No reason for either of us to get hurt over a horse."

She clasped the shotgun closer to her chest. She was out of her element here. Give her a spreadsheet of income and expenses with capital expenditures and depreciation figures thrown in and she was happy as a miser in a gold vault. Facing a man with a gun determined to get back the horse he abused was more Cole's area of expertise.

What would Cole do? Would he rush the man? Shoot at him with only two shotgun shells left? Engage in conversation, trying to convince the man to leave?

"Hey chickey, what do you say? Do we have a deal? I walk up this fucking mountain and you just let me pass. All right?"

Oh gosh. What should she do?

Wait it out.

Of course. She relaxed as her confidence grew. Cole would remain silent. The man was incredibly patient.

She watched the boulder so hard it started to look like it moved. Then something did.

The man took a cautious step out, keeping his hand on the rock. She had an excellent view of him and she didn't like what she saw. His whole demeanor screamed selfishness and carelessness. As she stared, she could see that what she thought was a dirty appearance was actually a hundred tiny holes in his clothing and skin. He had definitely been hit by rocks and possibly by some of the shot. Blood marked his bare arms and face. Part of her shuddered that she'd done that, but half of her rejoiced. She was shocked to find herself so blood-thirsty.

He looked up the canyon wall, past where she hid, toward the rim. He studied the top, obviously hoping Angel would show herself.

Idiot. Angel was smarter than that. Hopefully, she'd kept on running. The jerk below didn't deserve her. What he deserved was life in prison, but Lacey doubted he'd get that.

Reaching into his vest pocket, he took out a flask. His head moved slightly as he scanned the entire wall, probably wondering if she was still there. Then he opened the flask and took a swig.

Only a coward finds courage in a bottle. Adriana's words to her one afternoon came back to her. If that was true, she might be able to play on that cowardice. She didn't want that man taking even one step closer to her position. Looking around, she scrambled back and picked up a hand-sized rock.

She brought it to her spy hole. She'd have to make sure he was looking down when she threw it.

He took another swig then capped the flask and returned it to his vest.

"Okay, gal, I'm coming up." He waited another minute before he took his hand off the boulder he'd hidden behind. He stepped forward. The shale slipped out from under his foot and he tottered as he tried to stay upright, losing more ground.

She couldn't have asked for a better position.

Minutes went by as the man struggled to make some headway. Giving up, he rested against his boulder and took out his flask again, before wiping the sweat from his brow with his vest.

Lacey let her hand on the rock relax. Maybe he would give up and go away. But her gut said he would come back if he did.

When he put the flask away, he studied the canyon wall again.

She watched, afraid to make a sound.

His lips moved up into a grin and her stomach dropped. Oh sugar. Now what?

He walked back behind his boulder.

Lacey held tighter to the rock in her hand and focused

on where the man had disappeared. She listened intently, but couldn't hear anything past the pounding of her heart.

She caught movement out of the corner of her eye. A few rocks tumbled down the canyon about a quarter way up at the very end on the concave wall. She opened her mouth to breathe, her lungs too tight for her to take anything but shallow breaths as she stared at the place where the rocks fell. It was probably just a jackrabbit or even a desert mouse.

But even as she assured herself of that, her gut twisted. There was plenty of cover on that side of the canyon for him to hide behind. Unable to keep still another moment, she pulled her arm back and let the rock fly in that general direction.

The rock hit the ground ten yards below her and started numerous stones cascading down the slope. Some hit the area where she thought Ray was climbing, but not strong enough to cause an issue for him if he was there.

She could try to go down the other side, but she would be in the open while he had cover, and it would leave Angel vulnerable. Ray could continue over the rim and find her horse.

No, this was her best stance against him for herself and Angel. If he couldn't make the rim, he couldn't get to her horse.

Holy sugar, she hadn't loaded another shell yet. Reaching into her pocket, she pulled out the two remaining shells. Loading both into the shotgun, she wiped her sweaty hand on her jeans before closing the chamber. If she had to shoot twice, the second would have to be to kill.

Turning back to her view, she scanned the rocky side of the canyon wall, all the way up to the ledge she was hiding behind. No sound could be heard and no movement seen.

Keeping her finger away from the trigger, she grasped the gun tightly. She scanned the entire side, focusing more closely on the area above where the loose stones had fallen. For all she knew, he was still behind the boulder at the bottom.

Then a noise to the right caught her attention and she held her breath to listen. She didn't hear anything else, but when she glimpsed brown leather moving between two boulders half way up the mountain, she released her breath and shivered. Fear fueled her movement as she took aim, closed her eyes and pulled the trigger.

Chapter Six

Lacey stumbled back a step with the recoil as it hit her shoulder awkwardly.

"Holy fucking Christ!"

At the sound of rocks falling, she opened her eyes to find Ray sliding down the side, the boulders he'd been sneaking behind having moved, leaving an opening she could see clearly through.

Once he'd found more cover, he yelled out. "Listen, girl, I just want the horse. I don't give a fuck about you!"

No kidding. All he cared about was himself. She didn't answer. Instead, she sat on the ground and forced herself to let go of the shotgun. How much longer were they going to play this game. She only had one more shell. What if she shot to kill him and missed? What if she didn't?

She licked her dry lips, wishing she had the bottle of water she'd stashed in Angel's saddlebags. Some Christmas Day this was turning out to be. She clasped her hands together, her nerves stretched as far as they could go. Why couldn't Cole come home early? She looked at her watch. It wasn't even ten-thirty yet. Once he got home, how long would it take him to find her?

She couldn't wait for Cole. She had to do something. Her choices were simple, hightail it up to the rim and try to outrun the man or kill him.

Unclasping her hands, she worked the soreness out of her fingers from holding the gun so tight. Some rancher's wife *she* would make. Her fingers were used to working a computer keyboard, not the trigger of a gun.

She rubbed her shoulder, only to find she had blood soaking through her sleeve. The recoil must have dislodged the stone. Cole had taught her how to hold the gun, but in her panic mode, she'd forgotten. There wasn't much she could do about the blood. Besides, it was already slowing.

She stood up, bringing the gun to her shoulder in the right position as she remembered her shooting lessons.

Line up the sight with the target. Take a breath, squeeze the trigger, and this time keep your eyes open. Lacey could hear Cole chuckle as he instructed her. She'd hit everything but the old trash can he'd set up as her target.

Keep her eyes open. Of course. She could do this. She froze. If she kept her eyes open, she would see the shell kill the man. She really didn't want to do that, but if he forced the issue, she had no choice. Finding her resolve cowering behind her appendix, she forced it out of hiding.

She could do this. She could do this. She could—what was that?

A single stone rolled down from the rim. "Angel?"

"I've been called many things, but never an angel."

Lacey swung the gun toward the husky voice, her finger found the trigger and she took a breath.

~~*~~

"Hey Cole, wake up."

Cole opened his eyes to find Clark standing above him. "What time is it?"

"It's a little after ten. How was the shift?"

Cole sat up and threw his legs over the side of the bed, but kept the blanket over his naked package. He looked past Clark. "It sucked. We had four fires."

The firefighter whistled. "Wow, that's got to be a record. When did you get in from the last one."

"About seven. Hey wait a minute, I thought you weren't coming in until noon."

Clark smiled. "That was the plan, but my kids were up before dawn too anxious to see what Santa brought them. Those little buggers went through their presents in record time and when they were done, it was more like 'daddy who?' So I figured since they were so into their new toys, I might as well come down and take my shift. I really appreciate you staying the extra hours."

Cole grabbed up his t-shirt. "I was happy to help."

"Well, I really appreciate it. If you ever need a favor,

just let me know." Clark headed for the kitchen where the scent of bacon and sounds of the new shift talking filtered in.

Cole's stomach growled. Yeah, he better grab breakfast before heading home. It would be a long time until his mother's big dinner. Lacey didn't expect him until noontime anyway.

He'd showered after the last fire, too gritty to wait, so he threw on a clean pair of underwear and his jeans and strolled into the kitchen.

He waved off a few "good mornings" and "Merry Christmases" and went straight to the counter where scrambled eggs, bacon, home fries and three open boxes of donuts sat lined up, mostly pillaged already. Filling his plate, he sat at the table where the men asked about the fires, having heard tidbits from the last shift as they left for home.

After satisfying their curiosity and finishing his breakfast, he filled a travel mug with coffee and headed out to his truck.

He'd just turned the engine over when his cell phone rang. The number was too familiar. He glanced at the clock. It was only eleven, so he turned off the truck and answered his phone.

"Merry Christmas, mother."

"Merry Christmas, Cole. Are you on your way yet?" She sounded excited. No surprise there. His mother loved her parties.

"I'm still at work, but about to head home. I thought dinner isn't until three."

"Oh it is, but I was hoping you could come a bit early. The Kahnes are going to be here and their daughter Hailey. You remember her, right?"

Vaguely. He'd barely spoken three dozen words to the woman in the last three years, but she was rich, and therefore, at the forefront of his mother's mind. "Yes, I remember her."

"Oh good. She is looking forward to talking to you again."

Really? His mother knew he was engaged. She just preferred to forget. Another reason he needed Lacey to come. "I'm sure she and Lacey will have a lot in common." He had no idea if they would, but it was one way to stop his mother's machinations.

"Lacey? Oh right. Anyway, I just wanted to make sure you were still coming. Your aunt Bonnie said that Trace said that you might be staying at your grandparents, but I knew that couldn't be true because your grandparents are coming here and everyone is so looking forward to seeing you."

Since when? His mother was up to something. "And I'm looking forward to seeing 'everyone'. Is there anyone special you have coming this year, I mean besides the Town Manager and Hailey?"

"Oh yes, of course Rafael is coming, but also the Brittons, and Mr. Greyson, and Senator Rodriguez and just maybe the CEO of Hanson Enterprises. When I told her you are a fire fighter, I swear she almost fainted. She so wants to meet you."

Ah, now the pieces were clicking into place. He was her show-and-tell this year. That's why all the pressure. "It sounds like a great dinner party. I take it I can't wear jeans then."

"Oh honey, you can wear whatever you like. Do you think you could bring your helmet? I'm just betting there's a lady or two who would love to have her picture taken with you."

"Sorry Mother. I'm not allowed to bring that with me." He'd just have to remember to take it out of his back seat before heading down to Orson. There was no way he was posing for pictures. Show-and-tell was one thing. Pictures brought it to a level he refused to go.

"Oh, I see." From the sound of his mother's voice, she was not happy with him. "But you are coming. You wouldn't disappoint me again, right?"

He barely kept himself from crushing his phone in his hand. "No, I wouldn't. I'll see you this afternoon."

"That's my boy. Kisses." The line went silent.

Cole threw the phone on the seat and stared at the firehouse. As much as he wanted to tell his mother what she could do with her party, she was his mother and he would do what she asked. But he wouldn't like it. His idea of leaving after an hour was becoming much more enticing.

If only they could have a simple Christmas dinner, just him and Lacey, his brother and his parents. But his mother's Christmas dinner, which she had catered, had become known far and wide, at least in Pinal county. She was queen bee of her little hive and she needed to stay on her throne. He just didn't understand why. Why was it so important for her friends and neighbors—

Cole stilled. Just like the woman at the third fire last night. His mother was like her. Now he understood why he'd lost patience with the single mom with two kids. Like her, his mother had her priorities messed up. That's what Lacey had been trying to tell him, but he refused to listen. It didn't change the fact that his mother was his mother and he had to do what was right, even if she didn't, but he could definitely see why Lacey was so upset.

Turning over the engine, he put the truck into gear and headed onto Copper Win Road. Relief permeated his gut now that he understood why he and Lacey could not agree. He'd just been too close to the problem to see it through her eyes. Now that he did, he was sure they could come to some kind of agreement.

Shit, when did Christmas become such a problem?

~~*~~

Lacey gripped the shotgun, focusing her attention on keeping herself from pulling the trigger before it was time. She told herself it wasn't Angel's former owner, but the scared part of her refused to listen. That a voice came from a boulder on the same section of the wall as herself had her in a panic. She could barely handle one man out to get her, she couldn't handle two. The husky voice hadn't sworn, so it wasn't him, but it could be someone working with him.

Yeah, right, Lacey. He just called on his cell phone in a place with no cell phone service whatsoever and asked one of his buddies to drop down from the rim without making any noise.

She licked her dry lips. Maybe her lack of water was causing her to hallucinate. Could a person hallucinate a sound?

"Are you going to put that thing down so I can come out, or are we going stay in this position all day?"

Her finger on the trigger tightened, but she caught herself just in time. "Who are you?"

"I'm Whisper."

Huh? Fighting her panic, Lacey stood straighter. She needed whoever it was to think she was confident. "Step forward, slowly."

She kept the gun level, her finger on the trigger, but when a tall woman with long, straight black hair dressed in a flannel shirt and jeans unfolded herself from behind a short rock, Lacey lowered the gun.

"You shouldn't lower your gun until you're sure I'm not a threat."

Lacey raised it again, her gaze drawn to the woman's high cheekbones and steel gray eyes. "Why are you here?"

The woman pointed toward the rim. "I heard the

shots from my trailer. Figured I probably should find out if it was tourists hunting or something else. From the way you shot at that man trying to crawl up this canyon, my guess is you're not hunting."

Lacey shook her head. "You live up there? I didn't think there were houses for miles around."

"There aren't." The woman stepped forward and placed her hand on the barrel of the gun and lowered it. "I don't like neighbors, so I set my trailer up there. So what's going on here?"

Lacey studied the woman who had to hunch over a bit to keep from being seen over the boulder cover Lacey could walk behind. She had a tan woven shoulder bag that didn't close and she wore a very worn brown leather cowboy hat. There really was nothing to lose by telling her. Lacey felt better just having the strange woman show up.

"Wait." She moved to her crack and looked below. "Crap, I don't know where he went."

The woman moved to another spot and peered down the canyon. "He's behind the boulder about a quarter way up on this side."

Lacey looked at the boulder but couldn't see anything. "Are you sure?"

The woman looked irritated. "Yes, I'm sure."

Something about her demeanor gave Lacey confidence in her. "My name is Lacey Winters." She held out her hand.

The woman shook. "I'm Whisper Adams." Her eyes

narrowed. "So now that we got that out of the way, want to tell me what's going on?"

Okay, so being nice wasn't one of the woman's strong points. "The man down there is trying to steal back his horse. It was taken from him after he beat it within inches of her life. My fiancé nursed her back to health and this lowlife came here on Christmas day expecting no one to be here and instead found me on Angel."

She paused and looked up at the rim. "Have you seen a white horse with scars and a trail saddle?"

Whisper hesitated, but then she nodded.

Lacey's heart beat easier. "Oh, good. She's afraid of people, especially men. I hope I can find her when this is over."

The sound of rock falling caused them both to look out at the hillside. Ray scrambled behind another boulder, much closer than before. Lacey leaned toward Whisper. "You don't happen to have a gun, do you? I only have one shell left."

Whisper reached into her waistband and pulled out a handgun. "I don't go anywhere without Sal. My rifle is up there though. I couldn't climb down here with it and remain unnoticed."

Before Lacey, could move, the woman stood, aimed and shot.

"Fucking bitch! I'm bleeding!" More grumbling came from below, but Lacey was too stunned to pay attention to it.

Whisper sat down. "I couldn't get much of him. The bastard is well hidden." She shrugged. "At least he'll be limping around the canyon. That will make his movements awkward and give me another opportunity to kill him."

Lacey grabbed Whisper's arm. "We can't kill him."

The strange woman stared at her as if she was some Native American ghost risen from the ground. "Why not?"

"It's wrong."

Whisper's grey eyes turned to ice. "No, what he did to that horse is wrong. That's torture. I'm offering him a quick death."

Lacey let go, not a little nervous now. "I completely agree with you, but we can't take the law into our own hands."

"Yeah, I guess you right." Whisper sighed. "If I killed him I'd have to move again and I like where we are now. Too bad. The earth is better off without his kind around." She studied Lacey. "So what's the plan? Injure him so he can't shoot, then get you back home. I'm assuming you live somewhere out here."

Lacey relaxed a little, glad Whisper had relented, but the idea of shooting Ray until he couldn't return fire had her stomach feeling queasy. Based on Whisper's facial expression, she looked forward to torturing him.

"I do live here. Actually, I think I'm still on our property."

Whisper raised her eyebrow. "I don't see any house. You must own a lot of land."

"It's not mine. It's Cole's and his grandparents. They operate a horse rescue ranch. That's why we have Angel. So far though, I've been the only one she would let ride her. I'm glad I went for a ride while waiting for Cole to get home or that man below us might have stolen her." She glanced down at her watch. It was only quarter after eleven. "My finance won't be home until noon. Even then, he won't know where to look for me."

"Then I guess I'll have to stay with you until he gets here. Unless our piece of trash decides to show a bit more of himself and I can take his gun from him. Since you only have one shell left, that won't do enough damage to make it safe to leave here." Whisper looked skeptically at her. "Or I could just leave if you don't like my company."

Something flashed in Whisper's eyes before she looked down, her hand gripping her gun tighter. Lacey's heart reacted. This woman had more to her than met the eye, and after a year of working at Poker Flat Nudist Resort where her boss hired only those who needed a second chance, Lacey recognized a damaged person hiding a good heart.

She smiled at the woman for the first time and laid her hand on hers. "I'm thrilled to have your company. I don't know what I would have done without you. Please stay."

Whisper didn't look up, but the tension in her

shoulders eased a bit. "I guess I can wait with you a little longer. If worse comes to worse and your man comes back in an hour, my guess is he'll be hightailing it out here looking for you." Whisper snorted. "After all, it *is* Christmas."

Oh boy, she wanted to know a lot more about Whisper. There was so much in her attitude that screamed she'd been hurt.

Rocks sliding down the hill caught their attention and they both moved to their view holes. Whisper raised her gun and shot.

"Ow! You fucking cunt! That's it!"

"Get down." Whisper threw herself at her.

Chapter Seven

Cole turned down the dirt road that led to the Last Chance Ranch. He hoped that he and Lacey could talk about the Christmas dinner issue calmly now. He didn't like that they'd gone more than a day without speaking. It was like wearing jeans that didn't fit right. It was bearable, but downright uncomfortable.

He glanced at the dashboard on the truck. It was only eleven. Maybe they could take a ride out to their partial house. That always put them in a good mood. Dreaming of their life together as man and wife would definitely help. That's what he would do. Suggest a ride to the house.

As Cole turned off the dirt road and under the ranch sign, he took in the truck and horse trailer parked on the ranch and his pulse rate increased. Either it was a horse in need or someone had come to buy one of his horses. Stopping his truck next to the trailer, he turned it off and jumped out. He was down to only six horses, two of which couldn't be sold, so if there was another horse, he had room. The question would be, how bad was it?

There was no horse inside the trailer, so he strode to the barn. Relief that there was no new horse stabled there had him turning and striding to the house. They must have a buyer then.

Excitement coursed through him. It happened every time one of his horses went to a new home. He wouldn't let just anyone take a horse, and trailer or no trailer, he wasn't letting any of them go today until he inspected where they were headed. He always made sure the new home was well equipped to handle one of his damaged beauties.

He took the steps two at a time and threw open the front door. After walking into the living room, he strode through the kitchen, but no one was there. "Lacey!" He yelled as he walked upstairs. Where was she? Where was the buyer?

Not finding her there, he came downstairs and strode back outside to check the corral. Only Sampson and Lightyear should be there. Sampson couldn't be sold and they were still working with Lightyear. He couldn't be touched around his face which made putting the bridle on tricky. He'd been stung over a hundred times by bees and his face was very sensitive, either that or he imagined it was. As Cole came within sight of the corral, it was clear no one was there.

What the hell? "Lacey!"

Still no answer. He swung back to the area of the dirt

yard where they all parked. Lacey's crossover vehicle sat there. Where was she and the owner of the trailer? His muscles tensed as his mind skittered toward crime scene-like possibilities.

Sprinting to the truck with the trailer, he threw open the unlocked door and rifled through the glove compartment for a registration.

Ray Norton.

Cole's blood ran cold. "Lacey!" He jumped up into the bed of his truck to get a better look around, but couldn't see anyone. His heart beat erratically as a hundred scenarios played out in his mind. Ray kidnapping her and taking her into the desert to have his revenge was front and center.

Cole whipped out his cell phone. He didn't give a rat's ass if he was panicking or if it was Christmas. Nothing was more important than Lacey. He dialed Detective Sean Anderson. "I just got home. Ray Norton is at my ranch and I can't find him or Lacey."

"Whoa, hold on, Cole. Remind me who Ray is?"

"The bastard I'm testifying against in an animal abuse case."

"Shit. Okay, don't do anything until I get there."

Cole froze at the sound of a distant gunshot, his heart squeezing his chest so tight he couldn't breathe.

"Cole, did you hear me? Cole?"

Finally, he forced air through his lungs." I just heard shots. I'm heading out."

"I'll call for back-up. I'm on my way."

Cole stuffed his phone in his back pocket and ran into the house. Going to the gun case, he grabbed a rifle.

The shotgun was missing.

Did that mean Lacey had it or had Ray taken it? Lacey always used the shotgun because her aim wasn't good. He had to hope she had the gun with her. He took a box of twenty bullets and stopped by the front door to get the ATV key.

Shit, it was gone. Billy better have left it in the vehicle. Throwing the front door open, he ran for the barn.

"Fuck." There was no ATV. Did Lacey use it to get away from Ray? He had to get to her.

He pulled a bridle from the tack room and looked around the stalls before remembering Sampson was outside. "Cole, you need to keep your head on straight." As he started out, he glanced back at Angel's stall. Empty. Pieces fell into place.

He ran for the corral. Ray had planned to steal Angel back, but Lacey took her first. That meant Ray had the ATV and was hot on her trail.

"Come on, buddy. I know you're not used to bareback, but every second counts." Once he had the bridal on, he vaulted onto Sampson's back and raced them through the open gate. He hoped Lightyear stayed nearby, but he refused to lose the seconds that it would take to close the gate. He had to get to Lacey fast.

As he and Sampson approached his partially built

house, he slowed to study the tracks. Sampson pranced, anxious to keep running. Luckily, it wasn't hard to pick up the trail. Ray didn't even attempt to hide where he was going, barreling through plant life like he mauled horses.

Another gunshot echoed off the walls of the valley. If he had to go by sound alone, he'd never find her in time, but the tire tracks were clear. Kicking the more than willing Sampson into a gallop, he focused on the trail, not willing to lose one precious second.

His and Lacey's last argument came unbidden to his mind. All over his mother's stupid party. And like an idiot, he'd taken insult, storming off and leaving her alone in the barn. She was the most precious thing in his life. He should have stayed and talked it out, even argued some more. Instead, it hung between them for more than a day and now… Cole swallowed hard, trying to keep the images at bay of Lacey lying on the desert floor, blood seeping from a wound, slowly feeding the dry earth.

He pushed Sampson, the underbrush passing by in a blur. At one point he had to stop and backtrack to catch the trail again. He kept Sampson at a lope after that so he could follow the tracks. If they went too fast, he'd lose them again. He couldn't afford another delay.

The tracks veered off and he knew where they led. "Hold on, Lacey. I'm coming."

Three successive gunshots rang out, chilling Cole to the bone. His panic exploded inside him at the sound.

~~*~~

Lacey hadn't even hit the ground before three shots were fired at the boulders they hid behind. Stones flew, one catching her in the leg, another hitting her in the forehead. She bit her lip to keep from crying out.

Whisper rolled off her and crouched, facing the sculpted monoliths that served as their cover. "That bastard."

A large chunk had been blown away where they'd been standing. The two of them were forced behind one section of rock now.

At the look on Whisper's face, Lacey's blood ran cold. "Whisper, what are you thinking?"

"Hey, an eye for an eye." She got down on her stomach and moved to the hole. Lifting her gun above the edge, she shot.

Lacey heard stone falling and Whisper looked over the break in their cover and aimed this time.

"Jesus fucking Christ." The rock cascade grew louder and Lacey moved next to Whisper to see that she'd shot Ray in his leg. He slid down the sidewall, only stopping when he hit a cactus.

Whisper lowered her head to aim and shoot again.

Lacey pulled her arm. "No. Stop."

The woman's irritated glare didn't intimidate Lacey in the least. She'd faced worse from the people in her own town when they thought she was an arsonist.

The woman scowled. "He's still moving. I thought you wanted me to wound him until he couldn't hurt you."

"No, that was your idea."

Whisper's eyebrows rose before she looked away. "Whatever."

Lacey dared a quick peek through the hole. Ray dragged his leg as he awkwardly scrambled to find cover. Movement beyond him caught her eye. "Cole." He was on Sampson and galloping toward her faster than a dust devil spun.

She looked at Whisper who was busy reloading her gun. "Cole's here. He's found us." Tears gathered in her eyes as relief washed through her.

Whisper took a look through the opening. "So he is. I guess you'll be okay now. Just as well, I need to get back to my uncle."

Lacey grabbed Whisper's arm as she started to crawl away. "Wait. Thank you."

The woman looked back at her. "Just make sure that worthless piece of shit gets put behind bars for a long time."

She nodded and let go. Whisper crawled beneath the opening, and then disappeared among some boulders.

Lacey carefully sidled up to the new break in the wall and looked to find Cole. Her heart pounded the breath from her at the sight. Cole galloped furiously toward the canyon wall, but Ray leaned against a boulder, his arm crossed in front of him as he aimed his gun at Cole.

Rage like she'd never experienced filled her body. In one quick motion, she grabbed the shotgun and aimed at the man's back. Taking the breath Cole told her to, she pulled the trigger, keeping her eyes open.

"Argh!" The man went down as if someone had pushed him from behind and stone flew everywhere.

Cole pulled up and jumped from his horse, a rifle in his hand as he ran to crouch behind some sagebrush. "Lacey!"

She stood in front of the hole and waved. "Up here!"

"Stay there."

She nodded and sagged to the ground with relief. She dropped the useless gun on the ground then started to shake. Had she killed him? He may deserve to die, but she didn't want to be the one who did it.

As her eyes filled with tears, she brought her knees to her chest and rested her face on her jeans. She didn't want to be a killer. It was bad enough being accused of arson, but what if she was accused of murder?

He started it. She wiped her eyes at the childish thought. The fact was, he started shooting at her. She was only protecting herself and Angel. She fisted her hands as she looked above her. Where was her horse?

"Lacey?"

She looked to her side to find Cole standing there. "Oh Cole." She threw herself into the comfort of his large arms.

"God Lacey, I thought I'd lost you." He crushed her to him, making it difficult to breathe, but she didn't care. His quick heartbeat beneath her cheek made her shallow pants worth it. He was warm, alive and…shaking? She squeezed him as tight as she could, his hard body making her feel safe again.

He leaned her back and stared at her face. "You're bleeding." He lightly ran his finger across her forehead.

She'd completely forgotten about the stone hitting her there. "It was just a rock that ricocheted. I think I got one in my leg too. Oh sugar, I hope it didn't tear my lingerie."

Cole's mouth quirked up. "You have lingerie on your leg."

She gave him a devious smile. "As a matter of fact, I do. It's part of your Christmas present."

"Shit woman, you being alive is Christmas present enough for me." He pulled her close again as if he couldn't quite believe she was still breathing. "Christ Lacey." His voice sounded gravelly. "When I discovered that bastard was here and you and Angel missing, my heart froze and then the gunshots…fuck, I couldn't lose you again, ever." He rubbed her back as if reassuring himself she was still alive.

"Wait." His arms stilled and he peered at her left arm. "God woman, you've got blood all over you."

She twisted to look at her injury. "That's what happens when you trade gunfire on a stone hillside."

The sound of sirens echoed against the canyon walls.

She stiffened. Would they take her away? On Christmas? She didn't want to know, but she had to. She didn't dare look at Cole, but her voice shook "D-D-id I kill him?"

Cole's chuckle vibrated his body and she looked up. "What?" Irritation burned through her that he could find her funny. "It's a legitimate question."

"Ah Lacey. You did quite a bit of damage, but no, you didn't kill him. Your shot sprayed and got some in his ass along with a few stones, but it wasn't a direct hit, at least, not that shot."

"Oh. I did everything you taught me." She let her shoulders sag. "Just as well. I really was trying to shoot him. He was about to shoot you."

"I noticed." He placed his hands on her shoulders. "I was so hell bent to get to you, I forgot about Ray. When he stood up with that gun, I was just about to jump off Sampson's back, but you took care of that threat for me." He studied her. "When I tied the man up, I noticed he was winged by one shot and I think his shin bone may have been shattered by another. Did you bring a handgun too?"

She shook her head. "No. I had help."

"From who?"

Her gut said Whisper wouldn't want to get involved. She certainly didn't seem excited about helping and didn't leave any warm fuzzies behind when she left.

"Lacey. What is it?"

"I don't think she would want to talk to the police."

"She?" Cole looked off into the distance. "I don't think she'll have much choice. Where is she?"

She shrugged. "I don't know. When you arrived, she left."

Cole studied her. "Left where?"

She pointed up. "The same way Angel went. Can we go find her now?"

"Absolutely not. I'm taking you home and getting you bandaged up. Angel will find her way. She knows where her food is."

"Hey, Cole!" Detective Anderson looked up at them. "Is this your animal abuser?"

"Yes. He probably needs an ambulance."

Sean nodded. "Is this your handy work?"

He looked at her and smiled. "Nope. I have one tough lady."

The detective whistled. "That's one way of looking at it. I'll take care of this trash, but I'll need to talk to you two."

"Is tomorrow soon enough?"

"Afraid not. This guy has really made a mess of my Christmas."

Cole turned back to her and squeezed her tight again. "You ready to head down? It's pretty slippery. How'd you get up here in the first place?"

Her heart constricted. "Angel."

He cupped her face in his hands. "We may have to start calling her Guardian Angel after this."

"We need to climb up there and check to see if we can see her." She started to shake as the adrenaline she'd been functioning on the last couple hours slipped away, leaving her exhausted and worried. "I need to know she's okay as much as you needed to know I was okay." Tears started down her face as what little control she had disintegrated. "I have to know."

She stared into his green gaze, willing him to agree.

Cole's indecision flashed across his face as his gaze flickered over her. She jumped on it. "Please, Cole."

"Ah Lacey. I'm so damn happy you're alive. I can't stand to see you so upset." He gently brushed away her tears. "All I want to do is get you home where it's safe, but I can see that will have to wait. But if we can't find her or her tracks right away, you agree to go home and let me take care of you and send Trace out here to find Angel when he gets home. Okay?"

She smiled and wiped away the rest of her tears. "Okay."

Hope rose strong, and she headed up the few feet of gravel as fast as she could. When her head cleared the rim, she halted. "Angel!" Her heart filled with joy. She scrambled up the rest of the way, happy when Cole put his hand on her butt and boosted her up over the top.

She ran to Angel and hugged her. "Oh sweetie, I'm so glad you stayed nearby." Her tears started again, but this time they were happy tears.

"I'm not so sure she did."

Lacey looked back at Cole. "What do you mean?"

He walked slowly toward her and leaned over to untie the reins from the Joshua tree next to the horse. "Someone tied the horse here."

"Whisper."

"Why do I need to whisper?"

Lacey giggled. "No, Whisper is the name of the woman who stayed with me and shot at Ray. She's not going to get in trouble, is she? I only had one shotgun shell left to keep him away."

Cole moved toward her and grabbed her to him again. "Shit, Lacey, now your repeating yourself. You should have never been in such a position." He held her tight, his eyes tearing up as he gazed at her. "You mean more to me than anything."

She wrapped her arms around his neck. "And you mean more to me than anything. That's why I shot at Ray. If he'd hurt you, I would have made him regret it for the rest of his life. Let's go home."

He nodded just before his lips claimed hers in a possessive kiss that had her knees weakening. When he finally broke away, she held on to him. "Okay, now you need to give me a minute."

Pride infused his voice. "Take all the time you need."

She grimaced at him, her nerves completely frazzled and tired.

He studied the landscape riddled with Joshua trees. "Where did this woman named Whisper come from?"

The change in topic took her a moment. "I don't

know. She said she lived up here somewhere and heard the first two shots."

Cole pulled her against him again. "Can you stop talking about gunshots until we get home? My stomach is still a mess from finding you gone and Ray Norton's truck and trailer parked in our yard."

Her throat closed at the thought of what Cole must have envisioned. She would have gone into major panic. She nodded.

"Good. Then let's go home."

Chapter Eight

Cole stood on the front porch and watched as Detective Sean Anderson started his car and headed down the dirt driveway. Sean was a good man even if he did make Cole leave the house when he became upset while Lacey explained what happened.

At first he just paced across the dusty yard, visions of killing Ray Norton with his bare hands sustaining his anger. It was only when one of the horses neighed that he was able to break away from his one-track daydream and do something more productive.

The warmed up meal from Selma that featured tamales, had not only tasted delicious but also served as a release after the morning's events. The peppermint stick ice cream finished everything off in a festive way. He was glad he'd invited Sean to stay.

The mystery woman, Whisper, made the event a whole lot more complicated, but Cole wasn't about to complain about that. According to Lacey, the woman saved her life. He didn't envy Sean his task of getting the woman's side of the story. First, he'd have to discover where she lived.

That was his biggest concern about Whisper. Where she lived. That was Williams/Hatcher property over the canyon rim and if she was on it, he could have a squatter issue on his hands.

The best result of Lacey's harrowing experience was that Ray's charges had increased to shooting with the intent to kill. Even if a good prosecutor couldn't get that to stick, there were plenty of other charges that would keep him behind bars for a long time to come.

As Sean's taillights faded, Cole turned and headed back into the house. The sun was already past its zenith on Christmas and he hadn't spent much time with Lacey all day.

His phone, hooked to his jeans, vibrated again. He pulled it off and looked at the number. Same one as the last eight calls. He dropped it on the love seat where it wouldn't disturb him. His mother could wait. He grinned. That was the right thing to do.

He strode into the kitchen where he found Lacey loading the dishes into the bottom tray of the dishwasher. Her enticingly rounded ass in a clean pair of faded blue jeans had his body taking notice.

Cole silently moved up behind her and pulled her hips against his growing erection.

"Oh my." Lacey wiggled her ass against him, making him harder.

He reached down and cupped her breasts in his hands, pulling her upright against him, the need to have her close too much to resist, even if her red button-down shirt and his denim one was still between them. He lowered his head and licked the edge of her ear. "I want you."

Her body shivered against him, exactly the response he'd hoped for.

Licking down along her neck, he found the spot where her pulse beat hard and latched onto it with his mouth, sucking hard. A hickey may be very high school, but he wanted to mark her, brand her as his. Somehow it seemed like the way to stave off the panic of almost losing her.

She leaned her head away, allowing him full access as her heartbeat sped up beneath his tongue.

He released her skin for an instant and licked the spot before sucking again, instinct driving him on.

Suddenly, Lacey leaned forward and brought her shoulder toward her head. "Cole, wait."

He reluctantly released his mouth, but he continued to hold her tight. "What is it?"

"Look. It's three o'clock. We were supposed to be at your mother's by now. What will she say when we arrive two hours late?"

He loosened his arms but didn't release her. "We?"

She turned in his embrace, but didn't actually look at him. Instead, she smoothed her hand over the fire department insignia on his t-shirt. "Yes, well, I did a lot of thinking on that canyon wall."

He swallowed his rage as the band-aid on her forehead reminded him of her danger. "You mean while being shot at, you had time to think?"

She nodded but still didn't look at him. "I did. I realized your parents may not be as bad as I had made them out to be in my own mind."

"You mean they aren't monsters?"

Her gaze snapped to his. "I never said that. You did."

She was right. He grimaced. "Maybe because deep down that's what I believed. I didn't realize it until I was on my way home, but my mother really does have her priorities screwed up. It took you, plus a misguided woman whose house was on fire, and my slow brain, to finally figure it out."

Lacey rested her hands on his shoulders. "But she's not a monster. Ray Norton is a monster."

Cole's heart constricted with anger and fear all over again. He squeezed Lacey to him. "You're right. And I almost lost you to him which is why I'm spending the rest of Christmas day alone with you…preferably naked."

She moved her hands to around his neck and pressed her breasts against his chest. "Maybe not completely naked." The sultry gleam in her eyes had his cock getting hard again.

"Am I to understand that my Racy Lacey may have a Christmas surprise for me?"

She wiggled her eyebrows. "I guess you'll have to discover that for yourself."

"That's exactly what I plan to do." Without another word, he scooped her into his arms and strode out of the house.

"Cole, what are you doing?"

He grinned. "I'm taking you out to the barn. I figure since you started Christmas with Angel, we should continue it there."

She kissed his cheek. "I think that's a wonderful idea."

With Lacey still in his arms he stopped in front of Angel's stall.

Lacey called the horse, but it just stood and looked at them as if they were crazy. "I think she is happy to have fresh food and water."

He remained there, watching the rescue horse as she lowered her head and took some hay into her mouth. His heart filled with contentment. He had a challenging career, a mission that fulfilled him, and the love of his life. He couldn't ask for anything more.

Lacey's featherlight kiss on his neck sent a perfect peace flooding through his body. He stepped back and strode to their special Christmas stall. Letting Lacey's feet touch the ground, he held her, looking into her eyes. "I love you."

She smiled. "I love you too."

A need to make her his forever filled him. "Let's get married."

She laughed. "I think this ring on my finger means you already asked me that and I said yes."

He grinned, unable to help it at the sight of her laughter. "No, I mean now. Well, not today, but right away. Nothing big. Just here with our family. Hell, even at our unfinished house with just a minister and two witnesses. I don't care, just soon. I want to call you my wife. How about New Year's?"

She stilled. He could see her brain thinking of details, maybe even calculating the expense. He didn't want her to think with her head but with her heart.

Quickly, he lowered his head and kissed her lips, nudging his way between them to possess her mouth. His tongue entwined with hers, tasting the lingering flavor of peppermint from the ice cream. She moaned and her body melted against him. His cock grew hard and he broke the kiss.

"What do you say? Will you marry me on New Year's?"

Lacey opened her eyes and the love in her gaze fed his need. She smiled wide, her eyes sparkling. "Yes. I'd love to start off next year as your wife."

He whipped his hat into the air. "Yeehaw!"

She laughed. "Oh, I have an idea."

Cole's stomach tightened with anticipation at the gleam in Lacey's eye. "About the honeymoon?" He winked, even as his mind raced to figure out how many vacation days he could wiggle out of his captain on such short notice.

Lacey's grin was pure mischief. "We can definitely discuss that, but I was thinking about the actual wedding."

"Yes." He raised an eyebrow and pulled his head back

slightly. This was a new side of his wife-to-be that he'd never seen.

"Let's invite our parents to the ranch for a New Year's Eve party. Then after the clock strikes twelve, surprise everyone by getting married."

Cole felt his jaw drop open. His mother would be furious with them for not coming to her Christmas party. She probably wouldn't even come if they invited her to a party they held. She was like that. If she heard they had married without her present, she would…

Lacey's smile faltered. "You don't like it?"

The possible scenarios started to converge. His mother does come and brings the Hailey woman only to be surprised by the wedding. Or his mother sends his father and is in tears when she finds out they married but dad tells her it's her own fault. He grinned. "Are you kidding? I love it! A surprise wedding. Lacey you are a genius." He lowered his head and treated himself to another taste of her lips.

She ended the kiss quickly. "So now that we've settled that, are you ready to unwrap your Christmas present?"

His disappointment over the short kiss was forgotten as his whole body tensed. "More than ready."

She pulled out of his embrace. "Good, because I have a Christmas stocking just for you."

He cooled, unable to hide his disappointment. "A Christmas stocking?'

Lacey laughed again. "Yes. It's a Christmas *body*

stocking." She unbuttoned her top button and licked her lips.

He swallowed as his mind conjured sexy images of Lacey, but as she slowly undressed for him, they were all replaced by the sexual reality of his soon-to-be wife. With his cock rigid and his heart full, he watched, his gaze never leaving each piece of red covered or uncovered flesh she revealed.

Yup, he was the luckiest man in the world.

Epilogue

Whisper closed the book she'd been reading. Uncle Joey loved *A Christmas Carol*, by Charles Dickens, but he fell asleep on her every year. It was always in the same place, at the end of the visit from Christmas Present. Maybe it was purposeful. Who wanted to hear about death on Christmas night?

She pushed the button to lift the head of Joey's bed up six inches. He slept better that way. Then she put the book on the side table next to his bed.

Quietly, she made her way to the door and lifted her coat from its peg. Shrugging it on, she stuck Sal in her waistband and pulled a Corona from the fridge. After popping the cap, she let herself out into the night.

The air was crisp. She sat in the Adirondack chair she'd made and looked up at the stars. Taking a swig of beer, she watched a falling star streak across the sky. She loved the peace of the desert. Everything had its place. Life was good.

The morning's events stole back into her consciousness. While cooking Christmas dinner and taking care of Joey, she'd been able to keep her curiosity at bay, but now, she had to admit wondering if Lacey had killed the bastard. She'd heard the last shot as she made her way home. Then again it could have been Lacey's man who shot the animal abuser. She had total confidence Lacey hadn't been hurt.

Whisper took another swig of beer. She'd never wanted to kill someone as much as she wanted to kill that man. She'd be the first to admit she didn't like people, but she rarely had the urge to kill. After seeing Sacnite's scars though, she'd felt that coming upon the man who had inflicted such pain had simply been karma and she was just an instrument of fate. Lacey sure as hell didn't have it in her to kill.

She wiped away the condensation on the beer bottle with her thumb. Whisper had to admit, if only to herself, she liked Lacey. She was honest. Didn't try to be something she wasn't. The woman certainly had good taste in horses.

While she would have liked to keep Sacnite, the horse would have become bored. It wasn't as if she knew how to ride. She was better having her wildlife friends who came and went as they pleased, but the visit of the horse and the adventures of the day had made excellent dinner conversation. Joey's eyes had lit with interest as she explained every detail. It wasn't often they had anything so riveting to talk about. At most, it was her weekly ventures into the small town. She nodded. Yup, the day had given Joey some great entertainment.

About to take another gulp, she stilled. Something moved beyond the lights of the trailer. She waited and watched.

Finally, a nose peeked from behind some sagebrush. "Come on out, Faust. I see you." She clicked her teeth and the scrawny coyote crawled forward. "Slim pickens out there?"

The coyote stopped three feet away and sat on his haunches. His eyes were wary but hopeful.

"You know, I just sat down."

Faust's ear twitched, but otherwise he didn't move.

"Okay, already." She really didn't mind getting up, but she didn't want him to know that. She was actually pleased to see he was still alive. He hadn't been around for a few days. Moving slowly, she stood then walked back to the trailer to open a side compartment that housed a mini-refrigerator. She imagined it was originally designed for tailgating or partying, but she used it for much more important reasons. She pulled out the meat scraps she'd been saving.

Returning to Faust, she held the plate out. "You want to check and make sure it's good?"

He stood, afraid to move forward but in need of food. Finally, he sniffed the air about a foot from the plate. When he reached his paw to topple it, she threw the scraps a few feet away. Faust bounded onto the pile and started wolfing it down.

Hmm, could a coyote "wolf" or did he "coyote" it down? She grinned and resumed her seat, setting the empty dish on the ground and lifting her beer to rest it on the arm of the chair.

She watched the coyote eat until every tiny scrap was gone before it trotted back toward her and sat.

"Sorry, Faust. That's all I have."

The coyote stared at her a minute then lay down on his haunches with his paws in front and lowered his head.

That was what she should do soon as well. She took a swig of beer, her mind drifting back to Lacey. Was she cuddled up with her cowboy all safe and snug now? Probably. Whisper didn't need a man. When she was young, she'd had Uncle Joey to keep the vultures at bay, but she soon helped with the chore of evasion and survival. Now she protected him.

The question that had bothered her all afternoon came to the fore. How far had Lacey ridden from her home to end up so close to their camp? Whisper really didn't want to move again, not when she had everyone in town trained. But if Lacey and her man were close by, that would be a problem.

Whisper tipped her head back as she swallowed the last of the beer. It would behoove her to take a walk tomorrow morning and discover exactly how close her nearest neighbor was. Despite what she wanted, it may just be time to move again.

"Faust, I'm heading to bed." She rose slowly, her empty bottle in hand.

The coyote opened its eyes and lifted its head.

"Be a good coyote and keep an eye on the place, will ya?"

Faust laid his head back down and watched her.

"Good boy. Have a good night." With that, she turned toward the trailer and quietly entered.

The End

Read on for an excerpt from Trace's Trouble

Chapter One

Last Chance Ranch, Arizona

Stop right there unless you'd like your head blown off."

Trace froze, bringing Lightyear to a halt as his gaze swung to the barrel of a rifle barely visible behind the single boulder amidst the Joshua trees and sagebrush. There wasn't supposed to be anyone out here except a woman with a trailer and so far he'd seen neither. Drug dealers? Coyotes? His right hand itched to grasp his rifle from its scabbard attached to Lightyear's saddle.

He studied the area past the rock. Were there more? There was no other place to hide so completely. He didn't see anyone else. One delinquent he could handle. "Just out for a ride." He smiled crookedly. "Enjoying the day."

"Then turn around and enjoy the day somewhere else." The husky voice came again, but the rifle barrel remained steady.

Whoever held that gun was in his element. Shit. First he's tasked with doing Cole's dirty work and then he has to come across some territorial drifter. He frowned at the remembered conversation with Cole.

"You want me to do what?" He tipped his cowboy hat up to stare at his cousin as if he'd just sprouted six legs and a long poisonous tail.

Cole had the decency to look uncomfortable and lowered his leg from the rail of the training corral. "I don't really have a choice. If she's been up there too long, she could claim the land as hers under the Arizona squatter laws. This Whisper woman needs to move her trailer off our land. You know the boundaries. She probably won't have to move very far. She's up over the rim of the north canyon."

Trace had little sympathy for the opposite sex, including his soon-to-be ex-wife, but he couldn't see kicking the woman off their land when she'd just saved Lacey's life. Didn't really speak of gratefulness to him. "Does Lacey agree with you?"

Cole started to turn. "It doesn't matter. It's what needs to be done."

Trace stepped in front of his cousin, not the least intimidated by Cole's scowl. "You can at least wait until after New Year's. Shit, with this kind of 'thank you,' you'll be lucky if the woman doesn't seek us out and kill us all in our beds."

"Just do it." His cousin stepped around him and strode toward the house.

There was no way this scenario was going to go well for Cole and possibly for the rest of them. To hear Lacey talk about Whisper, the woman walked on water, able to shoot a cactus bud on a saguaro cactus from a half mile away.

Trace pulled off his hat and wiped the sweat from his forehead with his bandana then stuffed it back in his pocket and lowered his Stetson. He liked Lacey. She seemed to be a decent woman, one of the few left. She was going to be fit to be tied.

His lips formed a slow smile. Now that was something he'd like to see. It would serve Cole right for being so ungrateful and sending him to do the dirty work. Trace looked back toward the corral to find Lightyear standing near him. Ignoring the horse's face, he patted its withers. "I guess you and I are going to cause some trouble, boy."

The horse shook its head to dislodge a fly, but Trace chuckled. "No, not for us, but for your righteous owner." He entered the corral and carefully bridled Lightyear. The horse was far too sensitive around his face, thanks to an encounter with a traveling swarm of bees.

His face had swelled so much he could barely breathe. His owner had left him for dead, but a caring neighbor had called animal welfare. Cole and his vet had nursed the poor horse back to health over a year ago, but it still couldn't stand having its face touched.

Once Trace had the bridle in place, he added the saddle blanket and saddle and cinched the strap. Patting the horse on his side one more time, he mounted.

"Let's get this over with, buddy." Trace kicked Lightyear into a trot and they headed out to the canyon. His cousin had a big heart for horses, but when it came to people who didn't tow the line, he had no give at all.

Too bad he hadn't had the same strict rules for right and wrong as Cole had. Instead, he'd been blinded by a love that wasn't reciprocated and lost everything he'd worked so hard for. He should have known. He would never get involved with a down-on-her-luck woman again.

In the meantime, he had a roof over his head and a job he enjoyed, most of the time.

Now wasn't one of those times.

"Today would be nice. I got better things to do than shoot and bury trespassers. Turn your fancy ass around and get out of here." Though the voice definitely sounded irritated now, he smiled inside at the man's confidence.

Careful to keep his hands still, Trace cocked his head. "I'm afraid we may have a problem. You see, this is my cousin's land and I'm not the one trespassing."

After a minute or two of no response, but with the rifle barrel still steady, he slowly moved his right hand down by his leg. The problem was, even if he did get to the rifle, he was a sitting duck up on Lightyear.

"Who's this supposed cousin?"

At the question, he stilled. Maybe he wasn't talking to a criminal. This could well be the husband of Lacey's Whisper. Preferring to settle the issue peaceably with no one getting hurt, most especially himself, he leaned forward in the saddle, hiding his right hand completely from view. "Cole Hatcher. His fiancé Lacey was up here recently."

"No she wasn't."

Ah, the man knew who Lacey was. Trace listened intently as a muted swearing and grumbling came from behind the rock. He couldn't quite make out any particular words except "hell."

Grasping the rifle in his hand, he gave Lightyear a tap with his right foot. The horse started to move forward.

"I said turn around!"

Trace moved his left hand toward Lightyear's face. "Whoa, it's okay, boy." He scratched beneath the horse's ear and Lightyear reared. Gripping the horse with his knees, he swung the rifle around and shot the rock where the barrel was visible.

"Dammit." The barrel moved then. "Freaking-a, what the hell are you doing? I could have shot you."

He still felt like a sitting duck, but since the man hadn't shot him yet, it meant he wasn't trigger happy. "Show yourself."

A laugh sounded from behind the boulder. A very husky, feminine laugh and Trace's pulse accelerated.

Read on for an excerpt from Cowboy's Match

Chapter One

Cole Hatcher ignored the yellow and orange streaks of the Arizona sunset and focused on the same colors rising from the burning building as flames moved with the breeze. He spoke into the radio. "Move the two and a half inch to the northwest corner."

Two firefighters lugged the hose toward the base of the fire at the edge of the partially constructed building. Not more than fifteen feet away was a pile of old barn wood just waiting to ignite.

Stepping back toward the engine, Cole received a nod from Mason, the fire engine monitor, before speaking into the radio again. "Tanker, is the dry hydrant hooked yet?"

"Almost." The reply was not the answer Cole wanted. They would need more water than an engine and tanker could provide, and the chance of the winds picking up once the sun disappeared were better than a horse getting loose through an open gate.

As if on cue, the whinny of several frightened horses

in the nearby barn caused him to tense. There was no way he would let the fire spread that way.

The radio clicked before a firefighter's voice came through. "We're hooked."

Cole breathed easier. As long as he had water, he could put this baby out. "Good. Stay with the tanker. I'll need someone to come over here and grab the one and a half inch with Clark." He watched as Clark unwound the hose, already heading toward the construction site that hid behind the smoke and flames of the fire's onslaught.

Glancing back to where the tanker was parked thirty yards away, Cole swore. "What the hell?" Coming up the hill along the dirt road his trucks had just rolled in on, were at least a half dozen golf carts filled with naked people.

He stifled a laugh. What'd they think this was? A campfire? A Wild West show? Did they plan to make s'mores? This would be a story to tell at the firehouse for sure. Still, as with all spectators to a disaster, it wasn't safe for them to be there. He silently wished he had a radio to communicate with the owner, who had enough sense to keep the resort guests from getting any closer.

For over a year, he'd been curious about the Poker Flat Nudist Resort, but Clark had been chosen to give the fire extinguisher class to all the employees before the resort opened three months ago, and Cole had no official reason to come check it out. Fighting a fire wasn't a good way to learn about a place. Whatever this new construction was, it was toast. His concern was with the barn and the horses and which way the wind would blow next.

An explosion from the fire shook the ground as flames shot into the air. "Shit." What the hell did they have in that unfinished building? The two men with the smaller hose lost their footing and fell, but since they hadn't made it to the fire yet, they were unharmed.

He'd be damned if he'd put his men in harm's way when no lives were at stake.

He turned toward the owner and motioned her closer, then faced the burning construction site. As the sky behind the fire turned a dull pink, the breeze picked up, changing the direction of the flames toward the open desert. Good for the horses, but not for wildfire potential. It'd been the driest summer on record. October temperature highs had finally dropped below triple digits and the nights were already getting cold, but there had been no rain during monsoon season.

Cole spoke into the radio again. "I need the two and half inch to lay down a curtain between the building and the open desert on your side."

"Got it." The two firefighters adjusted their hose and started a continual spray, wetting and cooling the area toward the open desert even as the men with the one and a half inch hose moved in to cover the fire base.

"Lieutenant, you wanted us?" The female voice had him turning around.

He'd forgotten he'd called over the owner. At least

she and the cowboy with her were dressed. "You need to get those people out of here. I can't control the fire's embers and right now the wind is picking up."

The tall man nodded. "I'll take care of that." He immediately strode toward the golf cart brigade.

Cole turned his attention to the woman. "I've got my men focused on keeping the fire from spreading to your barn or out into the desert. A wildfire would be catastrophic, but we won't be able to save the building."

She waved her hand as if it meant little to her. "I'm not worried about the building as long as everyone is safe."

"Have you accounted for all your employees and guests?"

"Yes."

Another explosion had Cole turning away to check on his men. A voice came across his radio. "What the fuck is in here? A chemical lab?"

Cole frowned. He'd never thought of how convenient it would be to have a meth lab out at a nudist resort. He'd make sure the police investigated the place in case there had been illegal activity.

He looked at the owner. "How many more explosions should we expect?"

She frowned. "We had one before you arrived, that's what alerted me to the fire, but there shouldn't be anything that would explode over there. The plywood for the roof was completed, but they hadn't even set the windows in yet. All that was there was whatever the construction crew left."

"Do you have electricity out there yet?"

She shook her head.

Shit. "Gasoline for their generator." He spoke into his radio again. "Possible gas containers."

A gust of wind compounded his problems and he quickly repositioned his men. A siren could barely be heard in the distance, but the red and blue lights of a sheriff department car reflected far into the desert. About time they got here.

Cole spared a glance to where the golf carts had been parked and was relieved to see only a few left, but he scowled as a young woman with golden hair moved toward him and the owner, a tray of food and drinks in her hands. Shit, didn't these people realize this was a working fire? This was dangerous!

A third explosion rocked the ground and he spun in time to see a gust of wind pick up the roiling flames and throw them toward his men. He pressed the button on his radio. "Fall back!"

One man stumbled backward, catching his foot on the old barn wood and lost his grip on the hose. The other firefighter struggled with it before he went down too.

"Fuck." Cole sprinted to his men, pulling them back by their coats as the flames licked at their boots. The barn wood caught, feeding the fire.

Once his men were out of harm's way, he tackled the flailing line. A loose hose was a danger in its own right.

"Lieutenant, do you want us on the wood pile?" The question came through his radio.

Cole slammed his body onto the hose before replying, "Negative. Keep that curtain up."

The two firefighters that had been blown down regained their feet and grabbed the hose. "Thanks, Lieutenant."

He released his hold. "Pull back and soak that pile. If the wind shifts again, I don't want the barn catching."

The men nodded.

Cole turned around and strode back to the engine. The two women were still there. This wasn't a movie. Didn't they have any common sense?

After checking with Mason to be sure the water pressure was steady, he approached his audience, irritation growing at the petite stature of the blonde. Someone so delicate didn't belong at a working fire, but like the owner, at least she had clothes on. "Ladies, you need to get back." He pointed to the rise the golf carts had congregated on earlier.

The blonde smiled. "Selma sent over churros and iced tea for your men in case they need something."

Cole's blood froze. *That voice.* He studied the woman and his heart stumbled inside his chest. Her shapely figure proved she'd grown into a delectably curvy woman as he'd always expected she would, but her face was almost the same, just more refined. "Lacey Winters?"

Her brows furrowed and her button nose wrinkled as

she peered back at him. Had he really changed so much in eight years? Yeah, probably. He'd been a bean pole last he'd seen her…the night he broke it off with her.

She gave up trying to figure out who he was. "I'm sorry. Do I know you?"

He should let it go. No need to dredge up the past. He had a fire to control.

His pulse went into overdrive. Another fire. It couldn't be coincidence. He scowled at her. "You should. I'm Cole, Cole Hatcher."

Even in the reflection of the flames, her face turned pasty white and he kicked himself for revealing his identity. All he needed now was a fainting woman to contend with.

"You two know each other?" The other woman leaned on one hip, her concern for Lacey evident in the look she gave him.

At the owner's voice, Lacey recovered her color. Actually, her face changed from white to an angry flush in a matter of seconds. It reminded him of a flashover.

"Not that I want to know him." Lacey handed the tray over to the owner and stepped up to him. She poked her index finger into his chest. Hard. "So, Cole Hatcher. Are you going to accuse me of setting this fire? After all, I'm here, on the same property. It's not like you need evidence or anything. Feel free to assume the worst. I'm sure it helps to justify the way you treated me." She pulled back as if touching him made her feel sick. "Good luck with that." Turning on her heel, she stalked off, her hips swaying enticingly until he remembered where he was and who he was looking at.

"So *you're* the one who broke her heart." The owner studied him briefly then set the tray on the ground and followed after Lacey.

Shit.

For updates, sneak peeks, and special prizes, sign up to receive the latest news from Lexi at http://eepurl.com/D3MqT

Logan's Luck
(Last Chance Series: Book 4)
Dillon's Dare
(Last Chance Series: Book 5)
Riley's Rescue
(Last Chance Series: Book 6) *Coming Soon*
Aloha Cowboy
(Island Cowboy Series: Book 1)

MILITARY ROMANCE

When Love Chimes (Broken Valor Series: Book 1)
Poisoned Honor (Broken Valor Series: Book 2)

PARANORMAL ROMANCE

Masque
Passion's Poison
Passion of Sleepy Hollow
Heart of Frankenstein

Pleasures of Christmas Past
(A Christmas Carol Series: Book 1)
Desires of Christmas Present
(A Christmas Carol Series: Book 2)
Temptations of Christmas Future
(A Christmas Carol: Book 3)
One of A Kind Christmas
(A Christmas Carol Series: Book 4)

About Lexi Post

Lexi Post is a New York Times and USA Today best-selling author of romance inspired by the classics. She spent years in higher education taking and teaching courses about the classical literature she loved. From Edgar Allan Poe's short story "The Masque of the Red Death" to Tolstoy's War and Peace, she's read, studied, and taught wonderful classics.

But Lexi's first love is romance novels. In an effort to marry her two first loves, she started writing romance inspired by the classics and found she loved it. From hot paranormals to sizzling cowboys to hunks from out of this world, Lexi provides a sensuous experience with a "whole lotta story."

Lexi is living her own happily ever after with her husband and her cat in Florida. She makes her own ice cream every weekend, loves bright colors, and you will never see her without a hat.

www.lexipostbooks.com

www.ingramcontent.com/pod-product-compliance
Lightning Source LLC
Chambersburg PA
CBHW071003120726
47910CB00004B/1362